Dylan

Bowen Boys
Book 3

By

Kathi S. Barton

World Castle Publishing, LLC

This is a work of fiction. Names, characters, places, and incidents are products of the author's imagination or are used fictitiously and are not to be construed as real. Any resemblance to actual events, locations, organizations, or person, living or dead, is entirely coincidental.

WCP

World Castle Publishing, LLC
Pensacola, Florida

Copyright © Kathi S. Barton 2013
ISBN: 9781939865908
First Edition World Castle Publishing, LLC September 1, 2013
http://www.worldcastlepublishing.com

Cover: Karen Fuller
Editor: Eric Johnston

Chapter One

The house sat empty for the better part of the early afternoon, but now there was enough activity going on inside of it that she wished she'd remembered to bring an extra cell phone with her. Hers was being used for something far more important than recording the idiots in front of her. She didn't move from where she was hidden. If she did, any one of them could find and kill her. Jack Crosby wasn't going to die today if she could help it.

Glancing at her watch, she knew it was time to move. Pulling out her modified cell phone, she punched in the code to activate the small chip that hung around her neck. It had been in her head until recently, and she'd not been made aware of it until she'd gone to a friend of hers. They'd been afraid that whoever had put it there would know that it had been found and removed, but apparently not. Now she was doing her last job for these people.

Dropping to the ground from the tree she'd been in for over six hours, she stretched a little. Practice had made her able to stand the lack of movement, but she was still stiff. Moving along to the alley a street down from the target house, she moved in from the rear. The house was now as silent as a mouse.

1

Waiting until the last light was turned out, she thought about the chip again. Twice now in the past two weeks someone had set up an appointment for her to come into what they'd all called the shop and get a physical. The first time she'd missed it, she'd been in another country. She'd told them that she'd gotten food poisoning and couldn't make it back. The next time she had simply told them she was too busy. She had been, too. She was packing for her move out of the country again…this one permanent. Casey Snow, a veterinarian by trade and a good friend, had told her that she'd live longer if she left.

"Whoever put that sucker in you wanted to know where you were at all times. And now that I've removed it, they're going to want to put it back. Or maybe decide that you're too much of a risk now that you know and put some other piece of steel in you." She'd laughed, but Casey hadn't. "Do you know when they put that in there?"

"I'm thinking when I went to work for them or shortly thereafter. I had to go in for a physical, and I got my ass handed to me by one of the big boys when I was told to take him down. Of course, he was the third one they'd sent to me to show them what I had, but I was out and woke up in a hospital. The company hospital, not the normal kind."

Now it had been a few short weeks since she'd had Casey remove it, and she had been pulled from an assignment in Germany to come back and take care of a man she knew nothing about. And she was going in blind. Her assignment had one line and a single picture.

Kill the male and leave the others. Other what? His wife? Children? For as long as she'd done this work, she'd only killed one female, and that was because she'd been about to kill her and never any children. She had refused that from the very beginning. When the small device in her ear sounded, she made her way through the yard.

The light had gone off nearly twenty minutes ago. She knew that she was walking into a trap and hoped to Christ that they didn't have any idea that she was aware of them. She moved along the fence line and around the large pool. Jack knelt down in front of the security system and took care if it with a short break in the line. Moving to the door, she had it unlocked in less than four seconds. Opening it carefully, she moved into the house.

The kitchen had a jar of mayo setting out on the countertop, so Jack reached out and touched it and signaled to her that it was cold. Moving through the room, she saw that a set of stairs moved up from the back of the room. Ignoring them, she went through the dining room and into the living room. There was another set of stairs moving upward which she took, careful to hang to the outer part of them so that if they were squeaky she would more than likely miss them. But halfway up, she stopped.

She saw a spot of blood...not a great deal of it, but enough to let her know that she wasn't the only one in the house with her target. It smeared when she touched it with her gloved hand...it was fresh. Standing there, trying to decide if she'd had enough, she looked up and saw a shadow pass by what she thought was a window.

Moving up the stairs quickly now, she shot at the movement to her left as she dropped and rolled. The bullet that tore through her left forearm had her turning and firing to her right and dropping that person as well.

Jack moved to the open door, knowing that if there were indeed any more people there, they'd have to come from that room. The door behind her exploded when a shot was fired at what would have been her chest had she been standing.

Crawling into the room in front of her, she left the door opened and moved quickly to the other open door. But she rolled under the bed when someone came through the door after her.

"Jack, my girl, you might as well come out. We've got the house surrounded." She didn't move when she heard the voice of her boss, Kirby Mann. "I want you to know it's all your fault that this is going down this way. You should have left well enough alone and kept to the program. What did you think when you found that little piece of hardware in your head?"

Another voice mumbled, and Kirby laughed. "And so you know, we found your little vet. Too bad about that vicious attack from that cat she was caring for at the zoo. Tore her up something horrible. I'm sorry to say she didn't make it, either."

The door where she'd been headed moved, and a light nearly blinded her. She watched Kirby's shiny shoes as he moved around the bedroom until he was near where she was. Reaching down to her waist, she took out the knife and waited. It didn't take him long to rip the mattress off the bed and expose her.

"Got you." She heard the sound of a close gunshot and moved quickly. New pain in her arm made her breath catch, but it was going to be the least of her problems if he caught her. When she was jerked from the floor, she rammed the knife into his face and moved to the large patio door, firing her gun at them as she burst through it.

The pool was right below her, and she didn't hesitate to drop into it. She had a fleeting thought as to whether the cover was going to tangle over her when several shots were fired at her. Three hit the plastic below her, and two more caught her. As she landed, she heard screams and then more gunfire. As soon as the water went over her head, she blacked out.

Knowing that she'd only been out a few seconds, she waited, knowing that it would take them longer to come out of the house the normal way. She reached for the tiny air tank she'd shoved in her pocket at the last minute when she'd found out there was a pool. Preparedness was her middle name, and she was glad now that she'd found it in one of the little out of the way shops she'd visited in town. Lying as still as she could and using only her feet, she moved to what she hoped was away from the house.

She stopped when she touched the wall and heard someone speak. She waited, knowing that she was as dead as Casey if she tried to move now. When Kirby spoke, she knew that she'd hurt him but not killed him, more's the pity.

"I want you to get her out of that fucking pool. And when you do, you'll have to change her fucking clothes and drag her fucking ass back into the house. Mother fuck, this is a cluster fuck."

"Yes, sir, right away, sir," said a voice she didn't know. "I've talked to the hospital. They said for you to come in, and they'll…you're going to have to go in for them to remove the knife, sir. They said if it's that close to the eye, if you try taking it out yourself you might lose your whole eye."

Kirby screamed something she couldn't make out, and told the man that she'd fucking stabbed him in the eye, so he was pretty fucking sure it was gone. "And I'm going to make sure she pays for that, too."

The man who answered "yes, sir" sounded farther away. When Kirby spoke again, she realized that he, too, had moved. Touching the wall again, she slowly reached up to the side of the pool and lifted her head to look. No one was looking her way, and the one man who might pose a problem

Kathi S. Barton

for her was currently looking in the pool house. Moving now for the sake of speed rather than stealth, she pulled herself up and out of the water, and took off running.

She was just getting to the fence, a large wooden structure, when she was hit again. Her head felt as if they'd hit her with a steel bat, and she tumbled over into the lawn next door. Turning toward the house rather than away, she slipped into the doghouse she'd staked out earlier. Grabbing up the things she had left there, she tore off her wet things and put on dry clothes. Still dressed in the same fashion but with considerably dryer clothing, she slipped out of the makeshift changing room and got going.

Her head was pounding when she stepped in front of the target house again. Blending into the crowd of people that were gathering from the other houses, she moved across the street. She took off the chip and dropped it to the sidewalk, where it shattered. She picked up the pieces and put them into one of the many pockets on her clothing.

Jack moved up the street and toward her car. She was sick with pain, and dizziness was making her lose her way. Twice she'd had to back track until she realized at some point she was not anywhere that she knew. Walking because she knew they'd find her if she didn't, Jack moved along houses until they thinned out, then farther out until she came to a wooded area.

By the time the sun was coming up she wasn't sure of much of anything. That's when she saw the house. It had a light on in the back and one on the front deck. She made her way there and sat down on the swing, not really sure how she'd managed it, having blacked out again. She laid her gun across her lap and closed her eyes. She was going to die; she only hoped that she lived long enough to be able to convince

6

the person that lived here to bury her in the backyard and not call for help.

Closing her eyes, she let the blackness finally take her.

~~~

"I'm leaving now. I don't know how long it will take me to clean out my classroom, but once I get it done I'll come over." Dylan looked at his watch. "The longer you keep me on the phone, the later I'm going to be to dinner."

"All right, but you're going to be there, right?" He told his sister-in-law he would, for the tenth time. "I know you hate blind dates, but I didn't know until after Monica told me. I'm so sorry, Dylan, I won't do it again."

He knew she would, and so did she. He hung up the phone and made his way to the front door. He had had plans to clean out his classroom for the summer months, to get on his bike, and tour around for a while. He took a deep breath when he thought of the date he had tonight. He fucking didn't want a date. He wanted his vacation. Picking up the two boxes he had left to throw in his truck, he stepped out into the beautiful June afternoon. The first thing that hit his nostrils was the scent of blood, and a great deal of it. He turned slowly to his left when he heard someone clear their throat.

"I won't hurt you." He nodded at the woman sitting on his swing when she spoke softly. "I just need a minute. Then I'll be on my way."

Dylan set the boxes down and raised his hands. He looked at her and wondered if she thought that a minute was going to do her any good. The pool of blood beneath her and the swing was considerable. And the blood on her face looked like she'd gone a few rounds with someone who didn't care for her overly much. When she spoke again he asked her to repeat herself.

"Do you think I can have a glass of water?" Dylan nodded and moved to the door, only to have her booted foot come out to stop the movement. "You call the police or any other type of law and you'll never hear them crunch across your drive. Understand me?"

"Yes. I won't call the police. I'll simply get you some water." When her foot moved back, he could see what it had cost her to do even that small gesture. Blood didn't just drip now. It was a constant stream. He moved into this house and reached for his brother.

"Come to my house now. And have Walker bring his bag of tricks." Khan asked him what happened. *"I don't know for sure right now, but there is a woman on my deck bleeding to death. Oh, and she has a gun, so come through the woods. I don't need any more blood on my swing."*

Khan said he'd be there shortly, and Dylan grabbed a glass from the dish drainer and filled it with water and ice. He was about to leave his kitchen when he reached out to the windowsill and took down the bottle of pain reliever, only to put it back. Walker would want to work on her, and he didn't know what those would do to her if he had to operate.

When he came back out to the deck she was slumped over, but when he shut the door, she straightened up and looked at him. He could hear her heart beating slower than when he'd left her.

"I don't know where I am." Dylan told her his address. "That's pretty far, I guess." She looked out toward the driveway and then back at him. She was fading quickly now, and he was about to go to her when she looked at him again.

"Do you know me?" He thought she was asking if she had previously met him, but before he could tell her no, she continued. "I don't either. Know me, I mean. I can't remember how I got here, either, or why I'm bleeding. I mean, I've figured out that I was shot, but I don't know by who or why. I don't suppose you do either, do you?"

"No. I've never seen you before. And as for someone shooting you, I don't know about that, either. You have lost a great deal of blood, and you're probably going to die if you don't get some help soon."

She nodded and then held her head, using the hand with the gun in it. He was so focused on it he nearly missed what she said next.

"I don't know why, but I would prefer that you let me simply die, then bury me in the backyard." She fell back against the seat and he knew that she'd lost whatever battle she'd been working on to stay awake.

Dylan had to sit and slid down the post that was holding up the roof of his deck. He realized as he sat down that he'd been relieved that she hadn't shot him. When Khan entered his yard as his cat, Dylan couldn't even stand, but instead pointed to her.

"She's passed out. I don't think she's going to live." Khan went to her and touched his fingers to her throat. Dylan knew she wasn't dead but asked Khan anyway. He watched as his brother took her gun from her.

"It's slow. Walker was at my house when you called to me. He's coming in the truck. Should be here soon." He looked at the girl. "You think we should move her into the house or let him see to her when he gets here?"

"I don't know where she's bleeding from, and if we move her it might make it worst. Her head must really be hurting." Dylan shut up. It wasn't like him to babble, and he was afraid that she'd shaken him more than he knew.

"Did she tell you who she was?" Dylan shook his head and told him what she'd said. "Probably because of the crease in her head. She's going to have one hell of a headache when she wakes…*if* she wakes."

Walker pulled into his drive a few minutes later. Dylan was feeling better, so he stood up and greeted him. His dad and mom poured out of the next vehicle that pulled up. Dylan glared at his brother.

"They were coming up the drive when I left. I told them I was coming here, and she took one look at my bag and followed. What would you have had me do, tell them no? Well, good luck with that."

Walker came up to the girl slowly. Dylan didn't blame him; even unarmed she still looked dangerous. Walker asked to have help moving her to the floor so he could look at her to see if he could have her moved to the hospital.

"We can't take her there." Everyone looked at him. "She said that if she died she wanted me to bury her in the backyard. I'm pretty sure she knew she was dying."

Walker nodded once and started cutting away her clothing. Her moans made him want to go and tear Walker away from her, and that surprised him more than anything. Instead, he went into the house to get a pail of water and some towels for him. His mother came in behind him.

"Do you know her?" He shook his head. "Poor girl looks all done in. I wonder how we'd contact her family. Did she ask you to do that for her?"

"No. She said she didn't know who she was or how she'd even gotten here. All she knew for certain was that she didn't want me to call the police and that she wanted to be buried out back." Dylan picked up the pail and handed his mother the towels. "She's probably some hit man for the mob and her target fought back."

He'd had time to watch her when he and Khan had been waiting. She had on heavy boots with a thick tread. He could see there were knives in both of them, in pockets he'd bet were made for them. Her pants were black, as were the boots. The tight material molded to her legs like skin. The shirt, too, was black and long-sleeved, with small hooks on them to hang over her thumbs. He knew, too, that those were specially made for her. The black cap she had on covered her head so that all he could see was the blood that had dried on her, and the fairness of her skin. He knew that her eyes were gray, as gray as the sky when it stormed, and that the gun she carried was a Glock, just like the one he had in his own house.

"She has been shot. Five times it looks like, and the one that hit her head is more than likely why she can't remember anything. The one in her forearm is a clean shot, and I'll just have to stitch it closed. The one here, in her arm, is bad, and the bullet is still in there. I'll have to operate to dig it out. But it's the two in her back that worry me. One entered here...." Walker pointed to her left side high on her body. "This one hit a rib or two, and I won't know until I go in whether or not the rib has penetrated her lung. But this one in her back is the worst. It looks like someone shot her in a downward angle, like she was well below them. If the shooter had better aim, he would have killed her. I honestly don't know how she's made it this far."

"Can you save her?" Dylan's dad asked. "And if you do, will her memory return?" Dylan shot him a glance, as he was wondering the same thing.

"I don't know, Dad. I honestly don't know." Walker stood up and picked up his bag. "We're going to have to have a table set up so I can operate. I would like it to be in the kitchen, but I know that you've only just started remodeling the rest of the house and I can't have saw dust—"

"It's done. The cabinets were hung yesterday. I had a crew clean it up last night. We can use a few of the old doors

11

for a longer table in there. I have them on the back deck still." Dylan moved through the house, glad for something to do. When he brought the door in through the kitchen, his mother was standing there with clean sheets and a few of his older blankets. Together they made a makeshift operating table, then went out to help bring her in.

As soon as Dylan leaned down to help roll her to her back so they could get a sheet under her to carry her in, he knew what she was to him and it frightened him just a little. He tried not to stumble with her when they picked her up, but he tripped anyway. He looked at his dad when he tripped up as well.

"Watch it, son. You don't want to drop her this close to getting her all fixed up." Dylan nodded blindly and helped lay her on the table. He looked at his brother Walker and realized he'd been speaking to him.

"Dylan? Are you all right?" He nodded. "You'll have to leave. I need all the room I can get to—"

"I can't. I can't leave you in here alone with her." He tried to look away from him, but he was like a deer in headlights. "I can't do it."

Walker looked at the woman, then up at him. He nodded once and didn't ask him why. "You'll have to have a mask on and wash up. I don't think you'll touch her, but if you try to hurt me, I'll sedate you. Understand?"

Dylan nodded and went to the sink. When his mom came in to be Walker's assistant, Walker told her that they had it under control and that Dylan was helping. When they began, Dylan had to fight his beast for several minutes before he could see that Walker wasn't hurting her but helping. Walker looked at him.

"I won't hurt you. We won't. He understands that you're only here to save her." Walker helped him put on a pair of gloves and Dylan returned the favor, but grabbed his hands at the last second. "I don't want her to die. I know there's a good possibility that she's in trouble, but I can't let her die."

"I won't let her." And when he pulled out his knife to cut into her, Dylan looked away. He was going to stay with her if it killed him.

Chapter Two

"Anything yet?" Kirby sat behind his desk and waited for the man in front of him to answer. He didn't have a clue what his fucking name was, just some ass that worked for him. "She can't have gotten far. Hell, she was shot nearly a dozen times from what I saw."

"Nothing, sir. We've checked with all the hospitals in the area, as well as all the clinics and veterinaries. She's not shown up at any of them." He cleared his throat. "Maybe she found a hole and died in it. There was a lot of blood over that fence."

Kirby didn't answer but dismissed the man with orders to keep looking. The fucking bitch couldn't have simply done what he'd told her to do and entered the house from the front, where they'd been waiting for her. And she'd been nearly two hours early. The fucking cunt couldn't follow orders, and that's why he wanted her dead.

And now he had five people dead, including two of his own, plus he had lost his eye because of her. He picked up the handheld mirror he'd been looking in when his agent knocked. She was going to pay for this, too.

The knife had entered his socket and pierced his eyeball. The doctor who had treated him told him that he was lucky that he'd only lost an eye. The robber could have done a bit more damage than that had he pressed a little harder on the blade. Kirby had thanked him for his help, refused to stay overnight, and trashed the prescription on his way out. He had his own form of medication, and it wasn't anything this jerk would prescribe to him. Reaching into his top desk drawer, Kirby pulled out his coke and did two more lines of it. He was leaning back and feeling nothing when his phone rang.

"You want to tell me why there are nineteen agents pissing off about two dozen of my citizens right now?" said Marshall David, right hand man to the president of the United States, on the other end of the line. It took Kirby a few seconds to try and figure out what he was talking about.

"I'm sorry, what? You mean with the Crosby murder?" He knew almost immediately he'd made a mistake.

"I'm talking about the murder of Mr. and Mrs. Vern Clements and their lovely daughter Ruby. What is this about Crosby? Was that another family murdered?"

Kirby shook his head, then felt stupid as he realized that Marshall David couldn't see him.

"No, sir," Kirby said. "What I meant to say was that we're looking to connect a person by the name of Crosby to the murders." He hadn't meant to tell that yet, but he'd been too stoned to remember, and now it was out. "She worked for some underground hit crew until recently. But up until then we'd had her pegged as someone who we would watch but not be overly concerned with. Then last night she turned up in a house where one of my men was, and she killed him and the entire Clements family."

"Why?" Good question, Kirby thought, and was glad when he wasn't able to answer him. "I want what you have on her and this underground crew as soon as possible. Bring it to me yourself."

Kirby picked up the file to do as he'd been ordered when he realized that, as stoned as he was, he'd fuck up. He sat back down and tried to think how to get out of it. A glance in the mirror gave him what he needed.

"I'm sorry, sir, but I can't. I was hurt pretty badly last night in an attempted robbery. I only came in today to see what I could do to expedite this and find the murderer. I've been restricted to bed rest, but, sir…I knew that you'd want answers. Walking too much makes me dizzy and extremely ill." Kirby explained to his boss what he'd told his wife and the company doctor the night before.

"You should have told me first thing. I can't know these things without someone telling me. I'll have my aide come for the file. You go home. I have a feeling the shit is going to hit the fan on this one, and I will need all my good men with me."

"Thank you, sir, and I will," Kirby said, letting out a sigh. "I'll leave the file on the desk out front." He took down Marshall's personal phone number in the event he needed it, hung up the phone, and put the file on the front desk, not having a clue where his secretary had gone.

All Kirby wanted from the man was to leave him alone to do his job…not necessarily the one that Marshall had hired him to do, but the one that made him the most money. The underground crew that he'd hired to do the hits that the government needed done, as well as anything he wanted taken care of. And that's where the fucking bitch Crosby had crossed the line.

Kirby was about to leave his office when his aide came in with some news. He had to sit down to take it in after he heard the first part. The bitch had known about the chip for longer than he'd thought.

"The address we have on file is an empty lot. We checked it against the county records, and it's the same address she has listed there, as well. But to look at the place, it's been empty of anything for a while. The post office box is a fake, too. Casey Snow is the name on the mail. She can't be reached at her home. We're pulling records now to see if we can find her place of business. But according to the post master, her mail has been piling up for some time."

Kirby had a feeling that the body in her car wasn't Miss Snow but one stolen from the morgue. He wanted to scream at the man that he'd been duped but didn't. The only person who had known about the other woman was now lying on a slab in the morgue. He'd been one of the two men that Crosby had shot on her way into the house.

She'd had a great deal more street smarts than he'd first given her credit for. When he'd hired her over five years ago, he'd told her she was joining an elite team that only answered to two people: him and the president. Only the president hadn't known anything about this group, and Crosby had figured it out.

Crosby had been at the top of the list of candidates. Her tests scores were off the charts, and her IQ was well over anything he'd ever seen. She was also one of the most beautiful women he'd ever seen, with dark hair and light gray eyes, and she towered over most men, including him, in her stocking feet. He had known a few women that topped the six foot two inch stature, but no one had carried it like she did. Willow thin, she looked good in anything she put on, which was nearly always black on black. The one time she'd needed to dress up, the black evening gown looked as if it had been molded to her body. When she'd left the event, her target was taken care of and no one had a clue that the woman who had made heads turn was the one who'd taken him out.

But then she'd started asking questions…questions that he wasn't going to answer. When she'd removed the chip, they had made arrangements to have her taken out. She'd been one step ahead of them on that score, too.

He went home and walked into his house. Since yesterday afternoon, he'd been careful when he entered and left buildings. His house was no different. When his wife didn't come to see him as he walked into the living room, he drew his gun. Crosby was fucking with the wrong family if she thought she would get to his. When he entered the kitchen, he saw the note on the table and nearly picked up the phone to dial the police before he recognized his wife's scribble.

"Karrie had a dentist appointment, and I needed a few things from the market. We should be home around six, if not before. I'm sorry about dinner. Love, S."

Dentist. He put the note down and crumbled in the seat. Christ, he wasn't going to make it if they didn't find her soon. Kirby had to do something to protect his family, and he was making arrangements when his wife, Sally, walked in the door at a quarter of six. He was sending them away on a trip. As far away as he could send them. And they were leaving first thing in the morning.

"But I don't understand why you can't come with us." Sally took two slices of pizza he'd ordered for them and put it on her plate. "You've not taken a vacation in years, and this would be so much fun."

"I can't. I told you, if it wasn't for this thing going on at work, I'd go, and you know it. But with these murders and someone out there that might…I would just feel better about working these long hours if I knew that you and Karrie were safe." He ate his slices and reached for two more. "You and

Karrie go and have a blast. Call me occasionally and take lots of pictures."

By noon the next day, he was sitting in his office and his wife and daughter were on their way to France. He picked up the newspaper and nearly fell over in his chair. There it was on the front page: "WOMAN SUSPECTED IN MURDER OF PROMINENT LAWYER'S FAMILY'S DEATH."

Kirby read it twice and was relieved to see that no one had mentioned her name. If she got wind that they had anything on her, he'd be lucky if he ever even heard her name again, much less saw her. He wondered where the hell she'd gone and why the hell he couldn't find out one piece of information she'd given them that was true.

~~~

Dylan sat in the chair by the bed and watched her breathing. He'd been watching her most of the three days she'd been there, and was beginning to think she might make it. He looked up when Khan entered the room and sat down.

"You should go out and finish your classroom. Mom said you only have until Friday to get the stuff out or the school will trash it." Dylan nodded but didn't move. "I can sit with her. I won't touch her, I swear."

"I know you won't." Dylan stretched out his long legs and realized how stiff he was. "Caitlynne came by to take her fingerprints to see if we could find out anything about her. She said she didn't have any."

Khan nodded. "Walker told me. He said that she'd had them burned off with acid. It must have been painful."

The two of them sat there for a long while before Dylan told his brother what he probably already knew. "She's my mate. I have a mate that has five gunshot wounds and numerous other cuts and bruises. No fingerprints and no name. It sounds so surreal that it has to be true."

"Dylan, whatever is going through your head is more than likely wrong. You have to believe that. She could just be a woman who was in the wrong place at the wrong time, who will have her full memory when she wakes."

He looked over at the gun she'd had on her, along with all the other weapons. There were three knives, two guns, a thin wire that had been wrapped three times into a long cord, and a grenade. A fucking grenade. He looked at Khan.

"You and I both saw her that morning. She was armed and looked like one of those ninjas that you see in the movies. She'd been hurt, not because she'd been in the wrong place, but because someone had taken objection to what she was doing there. Christ." Dylan stood up to pace. "The fates have really fucked me over and given me a damned murderer for a mate, and we're going to be on the run for the rest of our lives."

"You don't know that." Dylan looked at his brother. "You don't. And there may be a great explanation for it, too."

"Who are you?" Khan flushed. "A year ago you would have come in here and demanded that I toss her to the streets and wash all signs of her from my life, and especially yours. Now you're in here spouting good news and a positive outlook. Don't get me wrong, I'm happy for you, but again…who the fuck are you, and what happened to you?"

"Monica happened to me. And you might want to find the silver lining in this, too. She might just be the best thing that ever happened to you."

Dylan looked at the woman. "Silver lining, huh? Okay. Silver line this, jackass. She is still armed better than the Secret Service that Warren has around him, which is good. She can protect him when he visits. The fact that she doesn't know her name or probably anything about herself means I can tell her anything I want and she'll have to believe me, because she doesn't know any better. I can—"

"That's not what I meant, and—"

"You said 'silver lining,' so shut the fuck up and hear it," Dylan continued. "I can tell her she's the world's greatest housewife, and tell her that the house needs to be cleaned hourly so that—"

He hit the floor. Khan was a big man and stronger than him simply because he was their leader, but Dylan was pissed off, which he figured gave him an advantage over him. As soon as Khan hit him in the mouth, Dylan realized how wrong he'd been. Khan was simply bigger. And none of the moves that Caitlynne had taught them were working to his advantage.

After several seconds: "You had enough?"

Dylan thought about shifting and taking his brother down, but his next words made him rethink that.

"You shift and so help me, I will grab that grenade and shove it so far up your ass you'll never shit right again."

Dylan believed him.

"I'm not letting you go until you think about the silver lining."

But he didn't ask to be let go. He lay there under his brother, who had both his hands jerked behind him and his knee in his spine. He knew that if he didn't come up with one silver lining he wasn't moving.

"She looks like she can take panther sex." His head hit the floor hard. "I can't think of anything with you pounding my body in the fucking floor. What the fuck would you think if that were Monica laying there? I saw her bleeding to death. Help me, for Christ's sake."

Khan let him go. Dylan didn't get up but only rolled to his back and stared up at the ceiling. He didn't close his eyes, because every time he did, he saw her on the deck with the gun in her hand…and then later on the operating table with Walker cutting into her.

"She has more bullet holes in her than the five we worked on. There is at least one in her leg, as well as in her back. There are numerous cuts on her that I figure are knife wounds. Some of them are still pink." He looked over at his brother. "I'm terrified out of my mind that someone is going to come here looking for her, and I can't protect her. What am I going to do?"

Khan looked at the woman, then at him. "I don't know, but I can tell you this; she's stronger than she looks or she would never have survived getting here. And even though her mind is scrambled right now, she knew enough to tell you not to call the police. For all we know, she could be just what I said, a woman in the wrong place at the wrong time."

Dylan nodded and stood up. When the door to the room opened, he felt his panther run along his skin to help him. His dad seemed to know this and moved back.

"Turn on the television. You have to see this." His dad reached for the remote, and after a few seconds of punching buttons without any progress, he handed it to Khan. "Damn it, why can't there be a button that says 'on' instead of nine hundred that say stupid stuff like 'list' and 'cbl'? What the hell does that mean, anyway?"

"Cable, Dad," Khan told him with a laugh. Then none of them said anything for the next several minutes. The news was on each station and blaring the same thing.

"…to date, all we have is that the attorney for the biggest trial of the decade, Vern Clements, was murdered on Sunday night along with his wife Cindy and their five-year-old daughter, Ruby. The police are asking that any information on this woman, Jack Crosby, be called into the hotline." A picture of the woman in his bed flashed on the screen. "She is considered armed and dangerous. If you know her whereabouts, the police are cautioning not to approach her but to call nine-one-one immediately and leave the area. Again, Jack Crosby is wanted in connection to the murders of Vern and Cindy Clements and their lovely daughter Ruby."

"Turn it off." Dylan took the remote from Khan and turned it off himself. "I need for you all to leave now. This is now too dangerous for anyone but me to be here."

"I'm your father, and I'll not leave until—"

"Dad, don't you get it? She's a murderer. She killed a little girl, and now the police are after her. When they find her here they're going to arrest me, too." He looked at the beautiful woman. "I can't let that happen to you. None of you."

They left a few minutes later. His mom had been making lunch for them all in his kitchen and stayed to make sure he knew how to finish it. She looked at him before she left, then hugged him.

"There might be something more to this than we know. Even more than the police are being told. She might just be a victim of someone's revenge." Dylan nodded. "Are you going to call the police on her?"

"No. I'm upset, not stupid. If they find her here before she wakes, I'll work from there. If she wakes and remembers something…well, I guess we'll play that by ear, too." He looked down at his mom. "She's my mate, and I can't let her be hurt more than she already is. I have to protect her, and if that means hiding her here until we can get answers, then that's what I'll do."

After she left, he went back up to the bedroom and sat next to the bed. He wasn't sure what the hell he was supposed to do, but sitting around wasn't going to get him anywhere.

Glancing at his watch, he saw it was almost one, so he went to his desk and wrote a note. Then he got in his truck and went to the school where he taught to get his things before it was too late.

His cell went off several times, but he didn't bother looking at it. He didn't want to talk to anyone, especially Caitlynne. She knew, of course, that the woman…Jack he supposed he could call her now… was at his house, and she was more than likely telling him to turn her in. He had no intentions of doing that, and he didn't want to argue with her about it.

Four hours later he was pulling into his drive. There were no cruisers in the drive, and he didn't get tackled when he walked up to the house. The stuff from the room could wait until tomorrow or later. He needed to check on the girl.

She hadn't been found, nor had she moved. Dylan sat next to her bed again and took her hand. She was cold. He rubbed her hand to give it some warmth.

"I don't know what I'm supposed to do with you. You barge into my life, bleeding on my deck, telling me that you don't remember anything. Now I hear that you've murdered a child. The adults…I started to say that I could tolerate them, but I can't stand the thought that you've killed. And a child, no less." When her hand was warmer, he put it under the blanket. "And maybe my family is right. Maybe there is an explanation for all this. I just hope to Christ you can remember it when you wake up."

Chapter Three

Caitlynne hung up the phone and stared at it. The man was lying. She had no idea why, but there was no doubt that he was. And even though she knew that he'd lied about several things, telling her that he'd found Jack's finger prints all over the house was the kicker. She looked up when Marshall walked in.

"You've heard, no doubt. What kind of plans do you have to get your family here? I'm sure you don't want them there with a killer on the loose." He sat down across from her as he continued. "I can have a car pick them up and bring them here, or we can—"

"She didn't do it," she said. Marshall raised an eyebrow. "For whatever reason, and I can think of plenty right now, I know she didn't kill the Clements."

Marshall leaned back in the chair. "Okay. So you know something. Something about this case that no one else…. How many of your family members know?"

"All of them. Not that she didn't do it, but that…. Maybe you should just take it that she didn't do it." His bark of laughter made her think he wasn't going to let it go.

"No, I don't think so. You tell me what you know, and I'll give you what I have. And maybe between the two of us we can keep your family out of prison. And you know me well enough to know that I'm true to my word." She nodded. "Okay, let's start over, and no bullshit this time. You know something. Spill it."

She reached behind her, pulled out two bottles of water, and handed him one. "She's Dylan's mate. He found her five days ago when she ended up on his deck bleeding to death. He contacted Khan and Walker. I didn't come along until they had already operated on her. By then Dylan had figured out who she was to him, and the rest have come together to protect her. I doubt very much the girl is going to be happy with all this macho shit they tend to toss around like it's their job. But there's more."

"So you know, and I'm sure you do, it is their job. It's just too bad that the females in their lives are just as macho." He moved to her couch, and she followed him. "What else is there? I take it you've spoken to the police?"

"Yes, and they referred me back to their source, the one that took over the crime scene almost as soon as the police got there. I just spoke to him." She shifted on the couch and took a deep breath. "Kirby Mann told me that he had to take the case, as Clements was his best friend."

"I didn't know they were that close, but I knew that they were working together on a few things. I think he is helping him with the trial for a good friend, Jerry Small. Did you ask the girl what she was doing there? Could that be why she killed him?" She shook her head. "Are you telling me that she didn't kill him for that reason, or that she didn't kill him at all?"

"She might have, for all I know. But Mann told me that her fingerprints were all over the house. And that they found a gun at the scene." Marshall cocked his head questionably. "He didn't mention any blood, and this girl had to have been shot while there. Walker dug out several bullets that match that of a service revolver. If Mann had only just showed up on scene, how did two of his men get killed? Then there's the fact that Crosby doesn't have any fingerprints. They'd been burned off some time ago."

Marshall opened his mouth and closed it several times before he simply stared at her. She knew he was thinking about the pain she'd had to endure to have that done. She had thought about it too. Acid burns were horrific, and to have done it to all your fingers would have been horrendous.

"You say this like you know. Why did you try to do a search with her prints? What did she say when someone asked her what had happened? And you said two of his men? I thought there was only one shot."

She nodded. "He slipped up. I don't think he even noticed, but I did. He's been telling everyone that'll listen that she killed one of his men, but when I asked him, he gave me one name, then called him another later in our conversation. I just checked around, and the man turned up in the morgue without paperwork. And I haven't done any checks yet because I need to figure out Mann's angle, but I don't think he worked for me."

"And the girl, what did she say? And don't think I didn't notice that you keep avoiding that question." Marshall was as tenacious as a dog with a bone. "Caitlynne, I want answers."

"She'd been shot five times. One of them creased her temporal lobe pretty well. The others, two in her left arm, one in her right upper side that broke three ribs, and then there was one in her back. Walker said that she'd been shot from a downward angle. And when he showed me that, I knew that she'd been well below the shooter, maybe as much as ten feet. I think she was jumping from a window when whoever it was shot her." She handed him a picture from her briefcase. "This is what she looked like after surgery. The one at her head,

Walker thinks that's why she has no memory. She asked Dylan when she got there if he knew her, because she didn't."

"Christ. Can I have the picture?"

She nodded.

"What is her condition now, and why didn't he call the police then?"

"Last report I had, she was still unconscious and not moving. He didn't call the police because she had threatened him if he did. She also asked him to bury her in his backyard when she died. She told him that, while she didn't know what happened, she didn't want the police involved." Her personal phone rang. "I hope that's Dylan. I've been trying to reach him all day."

She picked it up and told Marshall who it was before answering. "Where the hell have you been? I've been trying to reach you all fucking day. I have some news on the girl you should—"

"She's awake. About an hour ago." Dylan sounded pissed. "She doesn't remember who she is still, and she's demanding to leave."

"I'll be there in five hours. Don't let her go." Caitlynne hung up and told Marshall. "I have to go and find out if she knows anything and isn't telling Dylan, or she really doesn't remember. I have no way of knowing these things, but I want to see her face when I talk to her."

"I'm going with you. I'll call Warren and let him know. I'll go to the airport now and meet you there." She didn't even bother telling him that she didn't think he should go, but simply nodded.

Twenty-two minutes later they were leaving the airport, and Warren was with her. Walker hadn't come with her this time, and after making a quick stop by the house to pick up their son, they were on their way.

When they landed just under four hours later, the entire family was there, with the exception of Dylan. She handed the baby to his daddy and then hugged everyone. Monica was getting so big that she looked like she might pop at any minute. But she had six weeks to go, and everyone was worried about her.

"I don't know why. I'm perfectly fine for a woman carrying around an elephant on a trampoline." They both laughed as they sat in the back of the car. "I'm really fine. It's just hot, and the twins are making me hotter."

Twins. And no one but a very few knew the sexes yet. Caitlynne looked at George as he cooed over the baby. She was so glad that he'd forgiven her for not telling him the name, but they'd wanted to surprise him. Little George Walker Bowen was the pride and joy of all of them.

They pulled up in front of the house a few minutes later to find Dylan on the deck, waiting for them. Shit, the man was pissed, and even from as far away as she was, she knew that he was nearing his breaking point. She suggested that maybe he needed to run, and Khan nodded. She went into the house and up the stairs with Marshall. It was time to meet the new sister-in-law.

~~~

She heard the door open quietly and then shut. She wished the man would just do as she asked, and do it now. She spoke to him without opening her eyes. The light hurt too much.

"I don't want to hear another word about you protecting me. I don't care that you think there might be something special between us. I want you to call me a cab and help me to get into it, and you'll be okay."

"Do you know why he'll be okay?" She opened her eyes to see who had spoken. This man was different than the other

31

one. From…Dylan, he'd said his name was. She looked to the man's right and saw a very beautiful woman standing next to him.

"Are you the police?" The woman shrugged, and the man shook his head. "Well, that's helpful. Do you think maybe I could get one of you to shut that curtain? The pounding in my head is no match for it."

The woman moved to do it, and then both she and the man sat down. "I think it's best if I leave here. I don't know what is going on or how I got here, but I have a feeling that I'm not in the best of positions right now."

"You're not. There's a warrant out for your immediate capture. And you're considered armed and dangerous," the woman said. "Do you know who you are?" She shook her head. "Could you look at me when I speak to you?"

"I have a pounding headache, as I've said, and I don't know if I've worn glasses or what before coming here, but things aren't too clear, and looking out makes me ill. But if you want me to puke, then I can look at you." The woman laughed. "I'm glad you find this to your liking. I would really like to get up and punch you in the nose, but I think that all I'd do is piss you off, and I'd be here longer. Where is *here*, by the way?"

"You're in my brother-in-law's house. That's all you need to know for now. Do you remember your name?"

"Dylan told me it was Jack Crosby. I have no idea why he'd lie to me, so I believe him. What I don't believe is how he knows. He said that I had some identification on me. I have no idea why, but that doesn't sound right." She shifted her legs in the bed and tried to straighten up. "I hurt in more places than I think there are names for, so if I offend you in any way, you'll have to forgive me."

She felt tears on her cheeks as she let go a string of the most vile curse words she could imagine. Pain made her sick, and she was moving to throw up when she felt a hand on her head. She looked up briefly to see Dylan there. He said something, and she felt herself fade away with the pain.

The next time she woke, the room was dark. There was a small light nearby, but not enough for her to see much. She could barely make out the form of a figure in the darkness. "Who-who's there?"

"It's me, Dylan." He moved closer and sat on the edge of the bed with her. "You hurt still? Walker, my brother, is a doctor, and he said he could give you something more for pain if you wanted it."

She wanted everything he had for pain but knew that getting doped up was not going to get her out of there. She shook her head once then said no.

"I need for you to listen to me. You know as well as I do that there is no way I fell down a flight of stairs, or whatever, to get in this condition. I have to leave here as soon as…." She felt the tears again and hated herself for them. "I don't even know where the fuck I am."

"You're in my house in Ohio. I don't know much about you to let you know how far you are from your own home, but you showed up here two weeks ago, bleeding on my deck. Walker operated on you here. No one other than my family knows you're here. And you're safe." He reached down and handed her a newspaper. "This came out a few days ago. That's how I knew your name. It says here that you killed an entire family, including a little girl. The man that you supposedly killed is—"

"I didn't do this. I don't know how I know that, but I don't kill children." She wasn't as sure about the adults, but she knew that she'd not killed a child. "You're in danger. I can't focus on this much, but just from what you said, I'm being hunted, and if they find me here, you'll be in just as much trouble."

He looked away, then back at her. He was in the shadows, but she knew that he was good looking from when he'd been with her the first time. She wondered how a man with a wife—because there was no way that this man could have remained unmarried—could want someone like her in his bedroom.

"It's not my bedroom, but the spare. I'm just down the hall." She looked at him. "Yes, I can read your mind. It's an ability I've had since childhood."

She tried to think. He could read her mind. What the fuck was that all about? He could read her mind. Jack looked up at him.

"Do you know who I really am?" He shook his head. "So I could be that person in the paper and you'd know it?"

"No. Whatever is wrong with your mind, I can't touch it. It's been locked up tight. If I tried to access it, I'd run the risk of hurting you. I'm going to let it go. But I can see the memories and see your thoughts of things that are going through your mind since you came to on my deck."

She lay back and closed her eyes. "That man and woman from before…do they know who I am?"

"Yes, but only what they got from someone else. And Caitlynne, the woman, said that she's having doubts of what he said to her. She said that she doesn't trust what he's saying to be true about the whole thing."

Something popped into her head suddenly. "There was blood on the stairs. I…I reached out to touch it, and it smeared. But I hadn't…I hadn't done anything yet."

He stood up and went to the door. When he stepped out, she decided that whatever she'd remembered hadn't been good. Tossing back the blanket, she tried to sit up and get out of the bed, but he came back in with the woman again. She tisked at her, and told her to get back in the bed.

"You're a bossy thing, aren't you?" Jack moved to stand, and sweat popped out all over her skin. "I don't know what you think you know about me, but I have to get the fuck out of here. I have to save you if you don't want to save yourself."

"I'm Caitlynne Bowen." Jack looked at her, shocked. "I can tell by your face that you know who I am, and what I am. So let's get things straight between us. You, for whatever reason, are in serious trouble. Trouble that I may be able to help you out of. As of right now, you're under arrest and in my custody. And, as of right now, I will have you cuffed to that bed or have Dylan hold you there until such time that I can determine what involvement you had in the deaths of that family."

"I didn't kill the little girl. I don't know about the adults, but not the kid. I don't do kids." Caitlynne nodded. "I don't know…. You're with the CIA, and that means something to me. Something I should know."

Her head began to pound again, and she let herself drop back on the pillows. She looked up when another man came toward her. She remembered him as Walker, Dylan's brother, the doctor. When he pulled her arm toward him, he told her that he was giving her something for pain.

Nodding, she let him give her whatever he wanted. She heard Dylan speak, but he was too far away to hear. She looked up at Walker as the medication was warming her. She had to try twice to tell him.

"The company doctor put something in me. I can't…I can't remember what, but Snow helped me take it out."

"I'll tell my wife. Let it take you, Jack. The sooner you rest, the sooner your head will heal, and we'll be able to help you." He nodded and leaned toward her. "Dylan is a good man, and he won't let anyone hurt you."

She wanted to ask him who would protect Dylan, but the meds were kicking her ass. As she drifted off, she thought of the blood again and wondered what stairs she was going up when she'd seen it.

Chapter Four

Dylan moved all the boxes from his truck to the storage unit in the back of his garage. He'd put all of her clothes in the thing the first day, and now stuffed them into the boxes. He felt something bite into his hand, and reached into the pocket to see what it was.

He wasn't as computer savvy as his brother, but he knew a chip when he saw one. This one had been broken into pieces, but he could see that it was state of the art techno. He slipped it into a baggie that he'd brought from his class and decided to run it by Caitlynne.

She was just coming out of the house when he stepped up on the porch. "She's still resting. Walker said he gave her enough to put her down for a little while so she would heal. He seems to think the harder she tries to remember what happened, the harder she is going to fight to leave here. I don't think that's a good idea." He agreed with her. "So what do you want me to do?"

He handed her the bag. "I found this in her things just now. I don't know what it is, but I'm pretty sure you can find out. It looks like it's some kind of chip."

"It is. It's a tracking chip. They use them on dogs and cats to help owners find them when they're lost." She held it up to the sunlight. "You think this was in her?"

He didn't know at all and told her so. "She said that the company doctor put something in her, and snow got it out. You think Snow is a person and not a thing? Do you think that…I don't know…that she was in on something more than just this murder, and they used this to give her information when she needed it?"

Caitlynne looked at him and nodded. "I think that what we're going to find out is nothing compared to what she has in her mind locked away. I don't know why, but I have a feeling that something more than her simply getting shot is what will happen to her once they find her. She's the key to something huge. And just between the two of us, I got a feeling that Small is in on this, too."

The vice president had been caught in a huge sting two years earlier, and Caitlynne had been a big part of it. Dylan had been working and not able to go to DC where she lived to help out, but knew enough from Walker that the man whose job that Caitlynne had ended up getting was the one trying to have her killed. He asked her when his trial was set to happen.

"They're working on that now. His attorney is screaming for a new trial because of the exposure Clements's death is causing. If they don't come up with something soon, he may get it. Clements's house and his office were cleaned out of anything on the trial." She nodded toward the house. "I have a few things you should see before you go back up to see Jack. It's more about her prints being found in both his office and that of the incinerator at his work. They're trying to say she was working on her own because she was infatuated with Small."

"And what does Small say about this? I'm betting that he's denying any knowledge about her, isn't he?" She nodded. "So, she went to the office, ransacked it, then took everything she found on him and burned it. Then went to his house, murdered his entire family, then did the same to that place. And when the fuck was she supposed to have done this? While they were shooting her up? Maybe while she was bleeding to death? Christ, Caitlynne, you don't believe this shit, do you?"

"Nope. And that's where you come in." He didn't like the look she was giving him. Nor did he think he was going to like whatever she had going on in her head, and thought to see for himself when she spoke again.

"You're going to help me figure out not just what she knows but just how involved in it she really is."

He shook his head. "I told you, her mind is locked down. I can't go in there and see what she had without hurting her, and I won't do that to her. I think she's been through enough."

"You're right, she has, and I wouldn't ask you to hurt her. But Mann isn't hurt, and you can help me with him."

"Do I even want to know who Mann is and why you think he's involved?" She shook her head. "So you want me to go and touch this man to see what I can find out about my mate and if she's involved with the vice president. What if everything that they say about her is true? What if she's as guilty as the papers say she is?"

"Do you believe she is?" He didn't know and told her that. "Then this will help us all. If she's guilty, you haven't bonded with her, correct?"

"No, but that doesn't lessen the fact that she is my other half. What if I go...shit, I don't know... insane afterwards, and try to kill all of you for taking her away."

"Then I'll sic Monica on your ass. We both know that she is pretty good with a gun." Yes, he did know that. They had been working together to learn to shoot with Caitlynne, and not only had Monica been good at it, she'd done much better than he had.

He told her he'd help her and went into the house. He had more people there than he'd had since he bought the place. But the great part of it was, he was getting help on the house projects. He had already taken up the carpet in the dining room, and he'd been on his way out to get the flooring when he realized that the stuff from the school was there. He found Marc in the kitchen with the small chip.

"Somebody busted it," he said to Caitlynne. "I can read the serial number on it, but what do you want me to look under? I'm sure that whoever put it in her—if that's what they did—doesn't want anyone to know."

"I'm sure of that, too. So can't we just go in and see who manufactured this thing and not activate it?" She sounded condescending, even to him. Dylan laughed. "You have a better idea? Last I knew these things were being used to track animals. For all we know it could be from her long lost dog."

"She doesn't have a dog." She looked at him. "I'd be able to smell it on her, and so would anyone else in this house. She doesn't own a cat, either. Not yet, at any rate. And I think you should ask a vet, not look it up."

"Why?" Marc looked at the chip, and when no one answered him, he looked at Dylan. "Why ask a vet? I mean, I get that they would know, but how would they know why it was planted in Jack somewhere? And while we're talking about Jack, why would someone name her that? She's so not a Jack."

"I'll make that my first question to her right after we find out why she was shot to fuck and ended up on my deck." He tried to pull his temper in. "Sorry, but I don't like you thinking about her in that way. Hell, in any way. It makes my panther pissy."

Marc nodded. "I guess I can understand. I mean, having a mate can make you all sorts of possessive. Hey, look what just came up."

He'd found a site that specialized in using the tracking codes to find animals. All that was needed was the twelve-digit code, and it would bring up a map that would help track them, sort of like a GPS in reverse.

"I can try and fake a bunch of numbers and see if anything comes of it. Or, I can simply switch a few of hers around and see what I get." Marc looked at them both. "Or, you can see if anyone you know has a code on their pet, and we can use that."

"I could tell them I'm thinking of getting little George a pet and want to see how this works." Caitlynne went to the phone. "Now, who to call. I don't know anyone with animals."

"Surely someone in your office has a pet. Anyone. Hell, ask Marshall, he might have…no, he doesn't, either." Dylan snapped his fingers. "Dennis. I can call this kid in my class. He brought his dog in for show-and-tell, and was telling the class about this thing. Let me call. I'll just say I'm getting one for your baby."

Ten minutes later they had a code, and the map showed not only where the dog named Tinkers Damn was, but included a map of how to get there and a phone number to call if the dog had been found.

"The number is the same kind of system that's on this one. Seven numbers and five letters, and they are in basically the same format. So now we're pretty sure that this was used to track something." Dylan looked at Caitlynne as Marc asked the hard question. "Do we use it or wait?"

"Use it, but not here. We'll use the one in my office because it's a scrambled line. That way it won't come back to bite us in the ass if it is hers." She looked at the stairs. "Christ, I wish she'd remember."

"I wish my brother remembered that he was picking up flooring." Khan stood in the doorway, sweaty and covered in dust. "You should have been back nearly an hour ago, dumbass."

Dylan stood up and kissed his brother's cheek as he walked by him. He had no idea why he'd done it, and nearly lost a leg running from him when Khan set off after him. By the time he was backing his truck out, he was bruised and sore and had a bloody lip, because when Khan had caught him he'd beaten him to shit and back. Smiling, he knew he'd aggravate his brother again in a heartbeat. It was just too much fun not to.

~~~

Blood was everywhere. Jack was even swimming in it, her body weighted down by it. She tried lifting her head out of it, her lungs filling with the red liquid. The harder she tried to get out of it, the more it pulled her under. When she felt it break over her face, she screamed.

"I've got you." She fought against the arms that now held her. "Jack, it's me, Dylan. I have you. Nothing is going to hurt you. I've got you."

Clinging to him, she cried. She was safe. She had no idea why she'd feel that way, but she did. Holding onto him, she sobbed out what she'd seen. He continued to hold her.

When she quieted down, she felt stupid. She'd just cried like a small child, but when she tried to pull away from him, he told her to just wait.

"Your scream woke me from a dead sleep. I thought...Christ, I don't know what I thought. Then you started saying something about not being able to breath and that someone was trying to drown you."

"I'm all right now. I'm sorry. I had a bad…all that blood, it scared me." She didn't try very hard to get out of his arms, and he didn't seem to mind, either. "You should go back to your room."

"I can't. Caitlynne and Khan have it with the baby. And my parents and brothers are in the other rooms. Marc is sleeping on the couch. We worked late on the dining room, and they stayed over." He shifted around and lay down beside her. "You okay with me being here? I don't want to hurt you."

"I'm okay. It's your house, after all." She tried to think of something to say and went back to the dream. "I was drowning. I don't think it was blood, but a pool. I was in a pool somewhere."

"You know about what happened and what you're being accused of, correct?" She nodded. "There was a pool at the house where this supposedly happened. Maybe you fell in it or something."

"I jumped. I shot the window open and I jumped." Her body broke out in sweat. "Someone was chasing me. I don't…I can't…. All I can think of is an eye for some stupid reason."

Dylan nodded. "Are you hungry? My mom made some lasagna for dinner and there was some left over. Walker said you could have whatever you wanted but for you to be careful."

He stood up and walked to the door. When he went out and shut it behind him, she looked around. Flushing, she realized that she'd still been holding onto him, and he'd probably been freaked a little about it. She moved carefully in the bed and made it to the side without too much trouble. When he came back, if he came back, she'd ask him to move her to the couch and him take the bed. She didn't think he'd

43

do it. He seemed to be a really nice guy, but she was making the offer just the same.

When a woman returned with a tray, Jack tried hard not to show she was hurt. Thanking the older woman, she was surprised when she sat down in the chair next to the side she'd moved to. She smiled at her when Jack took her first bite.

"Dylan is talking to his brother. Every time you give him something he runs to them with it, hoping that it'll help. He said you were hungry."

"Actually, he didn't wait for me to answer him but hightailed it out of here without me saying anything." She took another bite and moaned. "But I'm glad he did. This is really good."

"Thank you." She reached into her pocket and handed her a clipping. "That was in today's paper. It says that Dylan was voted teacher of the year. His kids love him very much."

Jack read it as she ate. The portion she had was huge, so she only managed to eat about a quarter of it before she lay back to finish reading it. She handed it back to the woman.

"I'm assuming you're his mom." She nodded and told her that her name was Corrine. "Nice to meet you."

"You as well. I have pie if you want it. It's apple. It was all he had in the cupboards since he'd been working on the kitchen. You'll love it when he gets it all done. I think this is good for him to get his mind off of what is going on with you and all."

It took Jack a minute to realize what Corrine was saying. "I don't need to like anything he's doing to his house. As soon as I'm able, I have to get going. There are people looking for me, and I'm reasonably sure that dead or alive means whoever I happen to be with when they find me will also be killed. And when Company finds me again, they're going to find Casey."

Neither of them spoke. When Corrine started to stand, Jack moved to the edge of the bed and stood up as well. Pain moved over her like a freight train, and she had to hold on to the bedpost for several seconds to try and get it under control.

"I don't think you should be doing that. You've been shot several times and you've lost a great deal of—"

"I have to go. I have to get out of here right now." She stumbled for the desk where a gun and several other things were laying. "I'm guessing these are mine."

"Yes, but—" The door opened, and there stood Dylan and two other men, including Khan. "Thank goodness. She's leaving, and I don't think that's a good idea."

"Don't come near me." She picked up the Glock and held it in front of her when Dylan started for her. "I don't want to have to shoot you, but I certainly will."

"She's remembering." Dylan looked at one of the men. "Some of it is still fuzzy, but it's coming to her. Go get Caitlynne. She'll need to know this, too."

Jack moved toward them, circling to the right with her gun in front of her. She was getting sick to her stomach and hoped she didn't throw up. She'd had broken ribs before, and tossing cookies was not fun.

"Someone set her up. She hid in a tree for hours to see who or what they were up to and…. Snow is a person. Casey Snow. She moved the vet to another state until this is over, if it ever is."

"Stop that. Fucking stop that right now." She looked as the doorway filled with more people. "Being able to read a person's mind doesn't give you the right to do it. I want you to leave me the fuck alone."

"Jack, we have to help you. There are things going on, things you can't understand right now." Caitlynne spoke softly as she moved into the room. "Dylan needs to help you; he has no choice."

"Everyone has choices. And mine is to get the hell away from here." She took another step. "Please, you have to believe me. You're safer if I leave."

"You're going to have to convince her," Khan said. She looked at Khan when he spoke. "She thinks that she needs to leave so that you can remain safe. Show her that you can protect her if the need arises."

Jack watched Dylan move into the room, then the other men joined him. She looked at Corrine when they started to unbutton their shirts. This was just getting too creepy.

"I think you might want to sit down, dear," Corrine said to her. "This is about to become very frightening for you. Oh, and don't run. If you do, it will cause you problems, and I don't believe you need any more of those right now, do you?"

She shook her head and looked back at Dylan. The man had a chest that just screamed to be licked. When he winked at her, she flushed, then thought of shooting his dick off.

"Not nice. What will I do with you if you do that?" She flushed more when she caught images of them together in the big bed, and looked at the bed. She knew that he was doing that and tried not to think how enjoyable it would be. His low growl had her looking at him again.

The room tightened, and she had a feeling that all the air had been sucked out of the room. When she lifted her gun, she only raised it a few inches when she realized what had happened. The room was full of panthers.

"Holy mother fuck feathers." She stumbled back into the chair behind her as one of them walked toward her. "Stop right there."

He, of course, didn't. His paw was a big as her thigh, and she trembled when she could see the tips of his claws sticking out. He took it off her leg and laid his head in its place. Jack looked at Corrine and Caitlynne.

"I can shift as well, but I'm hoping that this will be enough to convince you that we can help you much more than you can do on your own." Jack heard the words that Corrine was saying, but it was too much. "That's Dylan on your lap. The others can't touch you because, if they do, he'll kill them. He won't want to, but it's in his DNA to protect you."

"Me?" Her voice squeaked, and she tried again. "Why me? I mean, I'm not a family member. I'm not even sure that I like you all."

He growled low, and she looked down at him. He rubbed his massive head over her lap, and she heard him purr. She looked up at Corrine again.

"You're his mate," Corinne said. Jack started to ask what that meant when Dylan lifted his head suddenly. She didn't know what was happening, but he looked tense, and it made her feel the same way. When the other cats moved toward the opposite side of the door, she knew whatever was coming was fucking huge. Dylan put his mouth over her wrist and held her.

"What the fuck is he doing? I need that." The cat that walked in the room wasn't as big as Dylan, and his black fur was tinged in gray. He looked older, softer, and a little heavy. The snort from Dylan made her look down at him.

"I wasn't going to shoot him." He let go of her wrist. "This is fucking off the charts insane, you know that, right? I'm going to wake up in a minute and this is all going to be a dream. I mean, there can't be four panthers in this house, in this room with me. I'm a reasonably sane person, right?"

She leaned back in her chair and stared at Dylan when he nodded at her. Standing up, she made her way to the bed. The sooner she lay back down and woke up, the faster this would be over. Dylan, the cat, crawled into it with her, and she didn't argue with him. Only insane people argued with figments of their imaginations.

Chapter Five

Dylan watched her lay there. He knew she wasn't asleep, but she didn't move, either. His family left the room as soon as she lay down. He remained his cat and stayed on the bed beside her. The first few tears hurt him more than he would have thought.

"I didn't kill that family. When I got there, they were dead already. I had an assignment to kill him, just the male, but not anyone else." She moved over more, and he nearly moved closer to her. "I know you think I should be happy about what you've done, showing me what you…fuck, I don't know what I think, but I'm still leaving. I'll tell Caitlynne all she wants to know, but after that, I'm going to leave. And I swear to you that no one will ever know what you've…that I was here."

He jumped down off the bed when she finally cried herself to sleep. Dylan shifted, pulled on some comfortable pants, and took her tray to the kitchen. Khan was sitting there with his mate and Marshall.

"She all right?" Dylan shook his head at Khan. "I'm sorry, Dylan, I thought it would help. I think it shows that she's a strong woman to not have run from the room screaming."

"She said she'd talk to Caitlynne and tell her everything, but she's still leaving." He turned to look at his brother. "I don't know what to do. I need her. I know that we've not mated or anything, but I can't let her go."

Marshall cleared his throat. "Actually, there is something you can do. Bite her. Well, not just bite, but you can mate with her. Do it tonight. I think if you do, she'll be more inclined to stay with you. Provided you do it correctly."

Monica laughed. "I think he's telling you there's more than one way to mate with her and it doesn't necessarily involve full-out sex."

Dylan flushed when he realized what she was saying. He looked at Khan, who was nodding. This wasn't the way he wanted to have her come to him, but he couldn't think of any other way to do it.

He looked up the stairs. "She's not going to be happy about this when she figures it out. And I fully intend to blame it on you if she means to shoot someone."

Marshall stood up and patted him on the back. "You do that. But let me know first. I'd like to show her what a pretty tiger I am first. She might like me more than you."

Dylan had been up and down the stairs that day more than he thought he had in a month. When he entered the bedroom, she was gone. Then he heard her cursing in the bathroom. He went to the door to knock, but she opened it before he could touch it.

"Is it too much to ask to take a shower? Wash my hair? I want to shave my legs and underarms, but I'm bound up tighter than mummies of Halloween." She tossed the brush at the counter. "I can't even brush this mop properly. I'm fucking cutting it off."

"I can help you." She looked at him as if she were seeing him for the first time. "With the shower. I don't...I would hate for you to cut your hair off. I love it."

"You don't have to fuck with it one armed, either." She looked at his hair. "You have really nice hair. I wouldn't think a teacher could have long hair like that."

"Normally they don't, but because I'm so amazing at my job, they cut me some slack." She snorted and looked back at the shower. "I really can help you. If you're worried about the wounds getting wet, Mom sponged them off daily and Walker said so long as they were dried well, it would be fine."

Lies, he knew, but he wanted her to be naked even if she was soapy and slick. His cock took a hard twist, reminding him that he wanted her anyway he could get her. Dylan moved to the linen closet and took out four towels. Then he reached into the stall and turned on the water.

"I can't get undressed." She licked her lips. "This is a really bad idea. I don't think I can manage this. Maybe I should just wait for a few more days."

He moved to her, slowly talking softly as he went. "I'll scrub your hair, and you can do the body parts. It'll be nice to be clean, won't it?"

She nodded, and he reached for her arm. The tape had been replaced so many times that it peeled off without much effort. When he had the wound in her forearm exposed, he felt a little lightheaded, remembering how badly she'd been hurt. He started talking to her as he removed the wrapping of her upper arm.

"When I was a kid, Khan and I decided it would be really smart to build us a race car. I think he was about ten, and I was six. So, without asking our dad if we could, or even if it was a good idea, we modified our wagon. Walker kept saying we were going to kill ourselves." He grinned at the memory

51

as he pulled the shirt she was wearing over her head and took the dressings off her back. "He was already acting like a doctor back then. He listed every bone we could break, starting with our necks."

He turned her around and pulled gently at the tape at her back. He was more concerned about this one more than the others. He tried to think where he was in his story and picked it back up as he pulled down the gauze.

"We had put cardboard around the edges. I have no idea why we thought it would keep us safe. Then we rolled it to the top of the hill behind our house. Thankfully, we'd gone there and not the street like I had wanted. But Khan had said we'd better make a test run first." He took a deep breath, bringing her scent into his lungs. "We can get you in the shower now."

Nodding, she went to the bathroom. He followed when she partially closed the door. Reaching in, she adjusted the water and then stepped in. Dylan opened the door wider and wondered how he was going to pull this off when, a few seconds later, her panties hit him in the face.

~~~

The water felt glorious. She stood under the hot spray for a few minutes before she felt someone touch her. She turned to stare at Dylan.

"I told you I'd help you." Looking him up and down, she turned away from him. Christ, the man was just too yummy for words. His small chuckle made her turn back to him.

"I'm not having shower sex with you. So if that was what you had in mind when you suggested this, then get the fuck out now."

He reached above her head. Her heart was pounding, and she was pretty sure he knew it. But other than showing her the bottle of shampoo, he didn't touch her.

"I told you I'd help you get your hair washed and cleaned up. I'm sorry I don't have anything but my shampoo, but I've never had a woman here before." She found that hard to believe. "I'm not saying I didn't have sex. I just never brought anyone to my home. It just didn't feel right."

His fingers started at her scalp and moved over her head in deep but gentle strokes. He massaged behind her ears, over her crown, and finally along her neck. When he told her to rinse, she was putty and had to brace herself by holding onto the tiled wall. Then, when he washed it the second time, giving her head the same wonderful all over touch, she had to lean her head against the tile in addition to holding on. Rinsing her hair out, she felt as if she'd been dipped in a total body wrap.

He handed her a sponge, a nice loufa, and then he squirted soap on it. He apologized again for not having anything but his scent. She nodded and worked the soap all over her body where she could. When he lifted her arm above her head, he said something, but she had to ask him twice what he'd said.

"Up or down? When you shave under your arms, do you go up or down?" She turned her head to look at him. "You can't manage this on your own. You don't want to hurt your arm, do you?"

"Up." She let him shave her arms and knew that on some level this was kind of weird, but had never felt so...so very pampered in her life. He held her to his body to shave under her left arm, and she felt his cock brush against her.

She stiffened slightly, and he murmured that he was sorry and pulled away. By the time he was finished, he had brushed against her three more times. She was beginning to think that this was going to get her into major trouble. And when he dropped to his knees in front of her, she backed against the wall. Jack watched as he rubbed the sponge up her leg, followed by the razor.

"We had it all planned out. Khan would do the driving and I'd be the co-pilot. Walker had come with us because he said that someone was going to have to get Mom when we got hurt." The razor scraped along her leg twice before he continued. "Turns out he was right."

"Dylan." She heard her voice and wondered for a second who had spoken so breathlessly. Her entire body felt as if it were on fire. She had to close her eyes or risk begging him to take her. It didn't help.

Every time the sponge moved over her leg she felt her muscles tighten. Then his hand would follow the path of the razor and she would melt again. He moved up and down her leg, over and over, until she thought she'd scream, begging him to take her. When he moved up her thighs, he asked her to open her legs, and she was glad they were in the shower. She was sure that had they been anywhere else he'd see have seen how wet she was.

As his hand moved over her smooth shins, his cheek brushed her thigh. Every time he moved along the inner part of her leg, she would anticipate him touching her. But he didn't. When he told her to turn so he could finish the job, she nearly sobbed in relief. But the tension only got more intense.

His chin touched the back of her knees, and she wobbled. When he lifted one foot up, then the other, and rubbed his thumb over the bottom of her feet, massaging her toes, she had to bite her lip. By the time he started to run the sponge over her calves, Jack knew that she was nearly to the point of throwing him to the floor and taking him.

"I broke my arm." Her mind was a haze of lust, her body on meltdown, and she had to ask him what he said. "I broke my arm when the wagon hit the tree. Khan only had a bruised head. When we hit the rock, I bounced out and fell on my arm."

His mouth grazed along her ass. His teeth nipped at her flesh. She couldn't move, couldn't breathe. His hands moved up her thigh, and she moaned his name. Turning around, she looked down at him.

His hand was wrapped around his cock. He moved up and down his shaft slowly as she watched him. When he stopped, she looked at his face.

"I can smell you. You are as aroused as I am, aren't you?" She nodded, not capable of speech. "I know you said no shower sex, but I would love to taste you. Sip from you until I come."

Her legs trembled as his head moved forward. Opening her legs for him, she curled her hand into his hair to hold on. When he suckled her clit into his mouth, she came, screaming his name. But he didn't stop.

His mouth ate at her. Devoured her until she was coming again. Every time she came, every time she exploded into his mouth, he continued to eat her, drink from her. When his finger slipped into her, she started to beg him. She had no idea what he thought of her, but she wanted him, inside of her, over her, and even behind her. He pulled away suddenly, and she whimpered. But he stood and took her mouth just as voraciously. His cock rubbed against her belly, and she reached down and wrapped her hand around him. He was so thick that she could barely touch her finger to her thumb. He tore his mouth from hers.

"Christ," he said, before cupping her ass and lifting her. "I need you. Please. Please, I need to be inside of you."

"Yes. Please. I need you, too." Lifting her higher, he brought her down hard onto him, impaled her over his cock, and she came again. When her back touched the tile, he pressed her hard against it, his cock throbbing within her.

"I can't be gentle. I can't…Christ, touching you like that, running my hands over your body like I did…. Then you came in my mouth, I thought for sure that I was going to come all over the shower." He moved into her, filling her over and over as he spoke. "I'm sorry, baby, but I can't wait."

He slammed into her. His cock filled her with every stroke. She threw back her head when he slid his mouth along her chin and to her throat. Giving her all to him, she wrapped her hand onto his head.

"Please," she begged him. "I need you to…please, Dylan, take me." His tongue licked the pulse she could feel pounding at her throat. His teeth scraped along her neck, and she tightened her grip on his head. When he sank his teeth into her, bit her hard enough to draw blood, she screamed again, coming hard enough that she saw stars dance in her vision.

He lifted his head and looked at her, his cock still hard and moving inside of her. Blood, her blood, dripped from his lip. His eyes, darker now, seemed to reach into her soul.

"Bite me. I want you to bite me hard and draw blood. Please, Jack, I want you to sink your teeth into my flesh and drink from me." She nodded and licked her lips. "Do it. Now, do it."

She licked his throat, not really sure she could do it, but when he commanded her again, the need to do as he asked—no, *demanded*—of her was overwhelming, and she did it.

Her teeth punctured his flesh; his blood filled her mouth. Sucking deeply, she moaned when his taste filled her. Drawing again, she felt his mouth do the same to her own throat, and she dug her hands into his shoulder and tightened around him.

They came together. Her body felt each stoke of his cock, his cum as he filled her. When he licked her throat, he pulled her from his wound and looked into her eyes. She was right, he could see deep into her soul.

"Mine. You're mine, do you understand that?" She nodded. "Say it. Tell me you're mine."

"Yours. I'm yours." He took her mouth again; his body took her as well. Even as he came again, she knew that things were different; that there would never be anyone else, and that this man was going to love her forever. As she came with him, his name sounding loudly from her lips, she knew that she didn't care at all.

He helped her out of the shower after he bathed her again. She was limp and a little sore. One of her wounds had opened. He ran his tongue along it, and she could feel warmth spread throughout her body. Then he did the same to the others, leaving a path of heat and tingling skin. Then he picked her up and put her to bed.

"I've never done anything like that before." She felt her face heat when he grinned at her. "I meant, I never had someone shave my legs before. You ever do that for a woman before?"

"No." He crawled into bed with her and pulled her to him. "But I wouldn't mind doing it for you again if you want. Touching you like that, holding you…I don't think I'll ever be able to shower again without you."

She was both embarrassed and happy. She tried to move away from him, but he wasn't having it. Jack had never slept with anyone before. Usually after sex, men couldn't wait to get away from her.

"Why?" She slapped his chest, then pulled on his chest hair. "I was wondering if you found me to be satisfying, and you're thinking about other men. Then you thought about that. I just want to know why they left you. I love holding you right now, all soft and sated."

"I'm not much of a snuggler, I guess." She shifted on the bed and looked up at him from his chest. "I don't do relationships well. Actually, not at all. The one time I came close to one, he left me at the altar. He slipped out the back of the courthouse with my friend. Not my best friend, just the only other female I knew. I think they divorced a few months after they married."

"I'm sorry about that. But I'm glad, too. If you'd been married to him when we met, I would have had to kill him." She waited for him to say he was kidding, but when he didn't she laid her head back down on his chest. "I'll never hurt you, Jack. Never. But you do belong to me now."

"I don't even know what that means. Belong to you how? I know I said I did, but…. Why did you want me to tell you? Like that? During…while we were…."

He kissed her mouth. "During sex? Because I can't fully claim you without your consent. And you gave it to me. Maybe…I don't know, I figured that you'd let me if it was in the heat of the moment."

"You tricked me." She started to get off him when he rolled her to her back. When she tried to hit him, he pulled her hands above her head and held them there.

"I need you. Not just for sex, but for me. I can't stand the thought that you hurt. I hate that those people who hurt you are still walking around as if they didn't harm something, someone that belonged to me. You do, too. Belong to me, now and forever. I need you."

She looked at his eyes as they began to change, lighten in the wake of his anger. She pulled her hand free, and he let her. Running her hand down his cheek, she saw him close his eyes, and she drew back and slapped him. He raised his head so quickly that she heard his neck pop.

"You ever trick me again, I will shoot you right in the dick. I'm not a child. I'm a grown woman who has feelings that get hurt when you do shit like that. You say I belong to you?" He nodded. "Then I'm assuming it's a two-way street."

"Yes. I've belonged to you since I first saw you bleeding on my deck." He rubbed his jaw. "You have a hell of a right."

"And a left, too, if you ever fuck with me again." She pulled his mouth down to hers and kissed him deeply before continuing. "Now go to sleep. I need my rest after that."

He laughed when he rolled to his back, taking her with him so that she was laying over him. She closed her eyes when she felt his fingers trail up and down her back in a steady motion. She was drifting off when she felt his hand slow then stop. His soft snore was the last thing she heard for a while.

Chapter Six

Kirby was sitting at home, enjoying his quiet time, when his phone rang. It was his personal phone. He was surprised when he didn't know who the caller was.

On the off chance it could be his wife or daughter, he answered with a laugh. "Don't tell me you miss me already," he said. "You've only been gone for less than a day. You didn't run out of money, did you?" He laughed again but realized no one was saying anything on the other end. "Sally?"

"I have her and your pretty daughter, too." His blood froze in his veins. "If you want to see them again, you'll go and find that cunt Crosby and bring her to me."

"Don't hurt them. Please, I beg you. Don't hurt—"

"You should have taken care of her when you had the opportunity. I told you what I wanted. I made it perfectly clear that she was to be dead. What did you do? You let her get away from you, and now she's out there."

He heard his wife scream in the background. Kirby stood up and realized he couldn't go to her, couldn't do anything because this man had her in his grip. He sat down slowly and brushed at the tears on his cheeks. He'd sent them away to certain death if he didn't find Crosby.

"I'm sending you help. He will be able to track her much better than any of you will ever dream of doing. You'll treat him as if he is me, an extension of me. If I hear one thing, I don't care how small, I will rape your daughter and have your wife record it and send it to you. Do I make myself clear?"

"She's only ten years old. Please, I beg of you—" The dial tone rang in his ear, but he wasn't through begging. "Please. Please, I'll do whatever you say, but please don't hurt her."

Kirby laid his head on his table and sobbed. He'd loved his wife more than he'd ever dreamed possible when he first saw Sally. She'd been standing with another woman at a fundraiser. She'd been wearing a dress that was very unflattering to her. The color made her look washed out, but when she turned to him and smiled, he fell head over heels in love with her just like that. Then he did again when, fourteen months later, she became his wife.

No one could believe how happy they were. Each time they were invited to an event, he would not leave her side, nor she his. Then a few months later, when she told him she was pregnant, he knew without a doubt that he was the happiest man alive. But complications set in.

She was dying. Three months into her pregnancy, and she was dying. The doctors had no idea why or how to treat her, but as she lay there breathing her last breaths, their unborn child grew weaker. Kirby had prayed harder than he ever had for anything. Then a man came into the room.

"You will owe me if I save them." The man said nothing else but stood near the bed that held Kirby's only happiness.

"What do you mean you can save them? The doctor said that they were both dying, that there was nothing we could do." He looked down at her, and then at the man. "Did you do this? So that I could owe you? Get one of your buddies out of prison? I won't be blackmailed like that. If you can save her, you damned well better."

He was up off the floor in seconds, his throat gripped tightly in the man's large hand. The man held him several feet up and looked him in the eye. Kirby saw his death and that of his wife and child there. It was as if he'd recorded it and was now showing it to him.

"Say you'll owe me and I will save them both." Kirby looked at his wife again and nodded. He was dropped to the floor, where he fell to his knees. As he stepped back to the bed, Kirby had a moment to wonder what he'd done. Then the man changed.

It wasn't his physical body that changed so much as his entire being. He seemed to grow larger, his face wider. When he opened his mouth, fangs dropped into razor-sharp points. Kirby stood up to go to Sally when the man raised his hand, and then Kirby couldn't move.

"I will take her blood and give her mine. The child will also have it through her link with her mother. She will not be as I am, vampire, but when I need her, either of them, they will come. You will be able to do nothing to save them."

"I've changed my mind. I don't want you to do this. Please. You have to—"

"It is too late." He seemed to strike at his wife's throat, his mouth covering her pulse. Kirby knew that he was drinking from her, taking away her blood when she was already so weak and could not afford to lose it. Then he lifted his head, his mouth covered in blood, and he licked his lips. Smiling at Kirby, the vampire bit into his own wrist and pressed it to Sally's pale lips. Whispering something in her ear, Kirby watched as she drank from him. After a few minutes he pulled away from her, and Kirby was sickened to see her reach for him again.

"I will require you to make some records go away. I want them destroyed, and any other information you find on a man by the name of Jerry Small. Anything," the vampire said, to which Kirby nodded. "I will come to you when I have need of you again."

"Again? I thought you said you only needed me to do this favor for her life." The man smiled again and shook his head. "You think I'm going to do whatever you want for the rest of my life?"

The man looked at Sally, who was watching the man hungrily. He looked away from her and at the man. He tipped his head at him and smiled again.

"You will, because if you do not, I will take from you what I have given. I never said that I would only ask a single favor of you. I said you would owe me." He took a step closer to Kirby, almost touching him. "And you do."

He had disappeared from the room, but not his life. Over the next ten years, the vampire had come by seldom, but always with a job Kirby was to do without question. He had learned the hard way not to ask questions. The knock at his door startled him from his memories, and he went to answer it.

"I'm here to help you. Lucius sent me." He bumped Kirby as he brushed past him and into the house. "I'll be staying in the master suite, and you can sleep down here."

"But I—" The man turned to look at him with a smile he'd seen Lucius use before. It said "fuck with me and I'll fuck you up." Kirby nodded.

"I'm a wolf, did he mention that? My name is Deveron. Anyway, I'll be looking during the evenings for that bitch that you let get away. I can't let someone see this giant wolf sniffing around, now can I? I like my meals to be brought to me on a tray and left outside the room. I want steak at least once a day, rare, and no vegetables. And chocolate. I love chocolate."

Kirby nodded, making notes on a scrap of paper he'd pulled from his pocket. By the time Deveron had finished, Kirby had two pages of his wants and a list of places to find the things Kirby had no idea how to get. But the one he knew he was going to have the most trouble with was the women.

Deveron wanted two a day. He wanted them on the plump side: "More to pound into, if you know what I mean" he'd said when Kirby had stared at him. He didn't, but said nothing. Kirby was also to call off work so that he could be at Deveron's beck and call. Kirby had already called off for that day, thinking to get the garage cleared out without the women there to pester him.

He thought he'd give just about anything to have them there doing just that. When Deveron went up the stairs to check out his new "digs," Kirby went to his office to call his secretary. She answered on the first ring.

"I won't be in for the rest of the week, Miss Black. I have caught a nasty flu and I don't want to waste my energy coming in there to not get my rest." She asked if she could get him anything. "No. I'm going to be fine. Just make sure you don't leave early because I'm not there, and no taking a longer lunch."

After hanging up with her, he made a call to the bar that Deveron had told him to get the hookers from. The man asked who it was for, and Kirby told him. The man seemed a little pissy after that.

"You tell him that if he hurts one of them I'm going to tell his master. I won't have him beating them to shit so they can't work. You tell him that Sheppard told you that."

"I will, sir. I promise." Kirby told him that he needed two women a day for an unknown amount of time. "And he would like them at the same time."

"He'll get what I send him and nothing more." The line went dead, and Kirby laid it gently into the cradle. He knew this man was going to kill one of the prostitutes and he was going to get blamed for it. Forty minutes later, someone was at the front door.

~~~

George watched the young girl at the stove. She seemed to be enjoying herself, so he sat still at the table and grinned. She had Dylan's scent all over her and she didn't even realize what had happened to her. When she turned and saw him there, she flushed.

"I didn't hear you come in. I was hungry and thought...you're Dylan's dad." He nodded. "Yeah, thought so. He looks like you. Want something to eat?"

"Yes, that would be nice." She filled a plate and handed it to him. When he started to protest at taking her breakfast, she waved him off.

"I'm doing this to keep from running. I want to." She looked at the door, then back at what she was doing with the bacon. "I've never been one to stick out a relationship, and this one has the markings of being more than a little bit over the wall strange."

"It doesn't have to be." He bit into the eggs and moaned. "Oh my, this is very good. I don't think I've ever eaten more fluffy eggs."

"It's the baking soda. Why can't he be like a normal person, a man? Why a fucking panther?" She broke four eggs into a bowl and started whipping them hard. He wanted to point out she was nearly at the meringue stage, but didn't.

"He is what he is…still a man but with a bit more." She snorted. "I don't think you believe me."

"No, I do. But if there was ever an understatement, that's it." Khan walked in and frowned at him, but George offered him a bit of his breakfast instead of speaking. Khan looked at Jack.

"I don't suppose I could have one like that, could I?" Khan sat down at the table as if she'd already answered him. "I could use some coffee, too, if there is any."

"I don't do coffee, and that machine looks like something from the next century. Have at it if you want any." She got another dozen eggs out of the refrigerator and another pound of bacon. "What kind of pack or whatever is this?"

George had his mouth full so Khan answered. "It's not a pack, but a group. Ours is a family, and that's what we go by. Packs are wolves. We're cats, not dogs."

"Well la de da, mister know it all. I was just asking. There was no need for you to get all pissy with me." She slammed his plate in front of him. "You should remember not to piss on the hand that feeds you, moron."

Khan opened his mouth and closed it twice before he sat and dug into his food. Before she could make her own breakfast another of George's sons walked in the door. Reed nearly hugged her when she offered to make him something, but backed off at the last second. She looked at him oddly but moved back to cooking.

"You know it's sort of hurtful the way you jerk-offs avoid touching me. I didn't do anything to that family. And I didn't kill that little girl." Her back was to them and she missed the look between them all. "I might be a lot of things, but I don't kill children."

"They didn't touch you because of me." George looked at Dylan when he came into the room. "You're my mate and they know it."

She looked at each of them, and Reed dropped his head, his face bright red. She looked back at Dylan and glared. George was glad he was there to see this. He had a feeling she was going to strip a hunk of hide off his son.

"You told them not to touch me? You actually told them that we had sex and now they can't come near me because of it? Why, you chauvinistic asshole." She slammed the spatula down on the counter and eggs went flying. "How dare you? How dare you treat me like I'm some sort of plague to them."

"I didn't tell them anything. They can smell me on you." George knew the moment she got it and so did the rest of them. Dylan was a little slower.

Jack looked at Reed, who still had his head down. She snapped at him to look at her. His head came up like she'd yanked it up. George felt a tightening in the room and looked around to see whose panther was showing. No one. He looked at the girl again.

"What do I smell like?" Reed looked at Dylan. "I asked you a question, not him. And you'll damn well answer me."

"Him. You smell like Dylan. And not because you used his crap in the shower either. You have his scent, the way his panther smells." Reed's nostrils flared. "And you smell like feline, too."

She looked at George. "What does that mean? And your answer had better be more helpful than his was."

"I would like for you not to speak to my dad like that." She glared at Khan and didn't back up when he stood. "You'll have respect for your elders, or I'll show you how to have it."

Her fist came out so quickly that there was no way for Khan to avoid it. When he started to lunge after her again, she pulled her gun out and shot between his feet. No one in the room moved.

"I'm a little stressed out right now, and you fucking aren't helping me by ordering me around and treating me like pond scum." She ordered Khan and Dylan to sit. "I've been shot up, beat up, and left for dead before, but I at least knew what the fuck was going on. You people are giving me just enough for me to feel like the rabbit down the hole and no tea party at the end to make it fun. And I'm not happy about it."

"No shit," Reed said very softly, but she heard him and took his plate away. He looked ready to argue with her, but she looked like she'd take him on if he did. Smart boy sat back in his chair and glared back at her.

"Now, this is how this is going to play out. I'm going to ask questions and you four are going to answer them. And I want the rip-the-bandage answers, not the millimeter–by-millimeter version. Got it?" Everyone nodded but Dylan. "You have a problem?"

"Yes. You're going to get your ass whipped when I get you alone. You don't treat my family like this and expect there to be no consequences." Dylan stretched his legs out in front of him as he continued his threat. "And then I'm going to have you apologize to them, each of them, for this."

"Fuck off. If I wanted to be treated like a five-year–old, I would have asked you to dress up like my daddy. I don't need this shit." She looked at the door again, then at them. "I'm twenty-seven years old, and single. I came into this world alone and as an orphan. My father died of a drug overdose, so I was told, and my mother did the same a few weeks later. I was delivered by c-section by some homeless man that had come across her. No one wanted a drugged-up baby, and I was one until I was a year old. I grew up on the streets as soon as I could escape the place I'd been put. You think you can threaten me and have *me* tremble in my boots?"

No one answered her, and Dylan even looked ashamed. He started to stand up, but he was stopped when she pointed the gun at him. He nodded once at her but didn't threaten her.

"You bit me, and that's how they knew not to touch me." Dylan nodded at her as she hopped up onto the counter. "And does this smell thing, will a human be able to smell it?"

"No. Unless they have some latent abilities, no one but another paranormal will smell it. To a cat you'll smell like another cat, but to other weres you'll smell off-limits. And when another male touches you, even human, I'll have an overwhelming need to mark you again."

"Mark, as in biting again or sex?" George felt his face heat up. She looked at him. "I'm sorry, but he started this."

"You go ahead and get your answers from us. You should have had this talk sooner. It's partly my fault. I wanted to see Dylan happy, and I encouraged him to see to you." George looked at Dylan. "Answer the girl, son."

"Both. The biting to mark you physically, sex so that I can dominate you again. Not that what we did wasn't mutual, but that's the way of my...our beast." She nodded. "If Reed had hugged you like he wanted, then I would have taken you back to the bed and fucked you until you couldn't walk. Next I would have sank my teeth into your cream flesh and marked you."

She reddened a little, but looked at Khan. "And what are you? You have some sort of power over the rest of them, right?"

"Yes. I'm their leader. Yours, too, now that you and Dylan are mates." She snorted again. "You will pledge to me or I won't be able to call you to me or you call me to you. I'm your leader as much as I am Dylan's. And your family, as well."

"Family I don't need. They'll get you killed." She looked at George. "And when you came into the bedroom as a panther the other day, why did they all run from you?"

"Run?" He tried to remember. "Oh no, dear, they weren't running. They were showing respect for the old man of the family. They gave me a wide berth to allow me passage. I've retired from the family as the leader, but they still have some respect for me."

"I'm sure they respect you more than a little." She hopped down off the counter and put her gun down. "This isn't over. But I refuse to resort to pulling a gun to get answers. You know something you think I might benefit from, you give it to me straight. I'm not stupid, nor am I some weak-kneed ninny that can only survive if there's a man around to save my ass."

Reed stood up and walked to her. When he pulled Jack into his arms, George looked at Dylan. His body was still, stiff as a board, but he didn't move to hurt his brother.

"I'm sorry, Jack. I really am. I'm not a mated male, so hugging you is sort of off-limits, but if you can take his wrath, so can I." He kissed her head, pulled his plate off the counter, and sat down. "Especially when you can cook like this."

George watched Dylan and the girl. He wondered what was going on behind their minds, both of them a study in stillness. When Jack turned back to the stove, Dylan sat up straighter in his chair and took a slice of bacon off Reed's plate.

"Jack, do you think I could have something to eat as well? I worked up a powerful appetite last night." She nodded but didn't turn around. "Jack?"

"I'm cooking as fast as I can. Maybe you should have taken into consideration how much you guys eat before you put in this tiny-assed stove." She turned and handed him a plate piled high with eggs, bacon, and toast. "If I have to do this daily, I'll want a bigger stove and a bigger refrigerator."

"I can do that." Dylan stood up and pulled her into his arms. "I'll do whatever it takes to make you happy."

George had a feeling Dylan was talking about more than the kitchen and nodded. This was going to turn out all right, and he couldn't wait to tell his mate. Corrine was not going to believe this.

Chapter Seven

Lucius watched the house from his perch on the tree. Deveron was proving to be much more of a problem than he'd asked him to be. When he'd told the wolf to make life difficult for the human, he'd never dreamed he'd make things this bad. He watched as the human Mann cleaned up the body of the woman that Deveron had murdered.

Lucius materialized in the room just behind the human. "He will pay for this. I did not give him leave to kill someone. He knows better."

The human turned and looked at him, shock written on his face. Lucius thought the human had aged much in the past few days, and it did not look well on him. When he turned his back to continue his task, Lucius tried to contain his anger.

"He killed her. Now I have to figure out what to do with her body and all the blood around this room. And that man…the one that sent her here…he's going to charge me for this one, too." The human turned to him. "Do you have any idea how much he's costing me to look for Crosby and not coming up with any more results than I did?"

Lucius swiped his hand around the room and the body disappeared, as did the blood and other parts of the woman. The human sat in the chair and looked around. Lucius thought the man was going to fall over the edge into insanity. He couldn't let that happen just yet. He still had a use for him.

"I will also take care of the wolf at the bar. You'll have no more problems with him." The human nodded. "Deveron has not been able to locate the woman. He says that you have given him false leads and misinformation. Is this true, human?"

"I've not spoken to the man but to tell him 'yes, sir' and 'no, sir' since he darkened my door. The little pisser even leaves me notes on what he wants me to fix him for dinner and when he requires another female or something." He looked at Lucius. "The only time he leaves this house is at dusk, and he returns within the hour without a word to me. If he can't find her, it's because he's not trying, not for lack of information from me."

Lucius had thought so. He moved out of this room and into the one below them by simply willing his body through the floor. He heard the human come down the stairs and sat to wait for him. When he came into the room that had the couch in it, Lucius bid him to sit.

"The girl? What do you know of her? Where she lives? Who are her friends?" Lucius knew very little about the woman who was messing with his plan, and hoped that when he found her he'd have something to hold her with.

"She gave us a bunch of half answers to questions, and the address she gave us is a fake. And the only friend she had has disappeared. I thought I had her killed, but it turns out that the woman in the accident had been dead for several days before the accident." Lucius didn't want to be impressed, but he was. "Crosby must have known we'd figure out she'd taken that chip from her body and had hidden the vet away so we couldn't find her."

"I don't know…. Chip?" The human nodded and told him what it was and how it had been used. "So she found the chip and had it removed. If so, then how did you know where she was at any given time?"

"She fooled us at first. I thought it had malfunctioned because it would work, then not, for a few days. I had set her up to have a physical done, a sort of head-to-toe look-see of her body inside and out, when she kept avoiding me. I had one of the tech guys look into her chip, and that's when I figured out she was controlling it on her own." The human smiled, pride in his voice. "She did a bang up job of it, too. Might never have figured it out but for the little glitch that we found when she went through the metal detector at work. It sent a double signal. She came there so seldom that we didn't catch it before."

"So she is smart." The human nodded. "I should have seen what I could have done to hold her in my services instead of you."

The human said nothing. Lucius heard the wolf coming back and waited. He told the human to go to his office and not to return until he called for him. Pulling shadows around him, Lucius sat quietly and waited.

Deveron was drunk. His body reeked of cheap liquor as well as women. When he staggered to the refrigerator and bellowed for the human, Lucius materialized. Deveron fell backward, only just catching himself.

"Lucius?" Deveron looked around, trying to straighten his clothing. "When did you get here? Come to check up on old Kirby? The man is not cooperating at all with what I'm doing for you."

Lucius nodded. "I can see that he is not giving you enough. How much progress have you made since I spoke with you yesterday?"

"I've just came back for some dinner. I didn't get a chance to eat before I left. There was a problem that old Kirby had to see to." He laughed, but Lucius remained serious. "He talk to you any since you've been here?"

"Yes, we had a nice conversation. Were you aware that he cannot lie to me? Unlike you, when he stuck a deal with me, it rendered him incapable of lying to me." Lucius had a chair move toward Deveron. "Sit."

The wolf sat, and Lucius stood up and moved slowly around the room. "Are you aware that wolf blood to a vampire is like a drug? It's like one of the finest wines ever made. And even as drugged up—"

"I swear to you that I'll find her. I swear it that—"

"Quiet." Lucius could smell the fear on the wolf; hear it in his pounding heart and rapid breathing. "I have given you several chances, Deveron. Many more than I have shown any other, wolf or human."

Lucius ripped back his head as he stood behind him, his eyes deeply bloodied red and his fangs long within his mouth. He leaned down, but stopped at the last second and felt the wolf relax, sagging a little in the chair. Lucius smiled and tore his throat out. Spitting his flesh to the floor, he came around the chair to face him as he died. Deveron struggled to live, but it was too late for him, much too late.

"I shan't sully myself with a lowly wolf like you. I'd rather starve. But fortunately for me, I had my dinner before I came here. You'll serve as a reminder as to who is boss. I will not have you or anyone else in my employment think that I am soft." Deveron's body dropped to the floor, the chair skittering across the room. "You'll be an incentive for them, I believe. An incentive for them to please me more."

Lucius called for the human and let him see what he'd done. The man sat down and didn't move, even after Lucius cleaned up his mess. He sat beside him at the table and had him look deeply into his eyes.

"I have put another wolf into service. He will help you, but will not bother you overly much. When he reports to you, you'll bring me the information and the girl when he finds her. I want her brought to me as soon as possible." The human nodded. "You'll bring her, then you'll end your life, for you've nothing to offer this world, and so long as you're in it, your family will know shame and heartache. Do you understand me, human?"

"Yes, sir. I will bring the girl to you and end my life."

Lucius left him sitting there and took to the skies. He had plenty of work to do and very little time to do it in. He had to have Small in the White House. He was going to be the key to so much, and he didn't even know it. As Lucius landed just outside the small, barred window that imprisoned this human, he smiled. This was going to be his greatest success.

~~~

Dylan spent most of the rest of the day on his knees in the dining room. They nearly had the floors put down, with only the little flooring that was left and the two corner cabinets yet to install to call the room complete. He glanced up at the antiques that he'd refinished during spring break. They were going to be beautiful in this room. He looked up when he smelled Jack. She looked at him strangely.

"Do you have to do that?" she said.

"Do what?" he asked.

"Look like raw sex all the time. I mean, is there some sort of meter you can turn down?"

Reed laughed but didn't stop pounding nails in the floor. Dylan sat up on his knees and smiled at her. She leaned against the doorjamb into the kitchen. She was looking better every time he saw her.

"I don't think that's possible, but if you wanted to keep me a little less stressed, I can think of a couple of ways for you to do that." She looked at Reed when his head came up. "Reed, go and find something else to do away from the house."

He moved like he'd been shot from a cannon, laughing the entire time. He kissed Jack on the cheek before he left, and she grinned at him. She was going to pay for that. Dylan took off his shirt, tossed it behind him, and stood up.

"Come here, love. I want to taste you," he said. She shook her head. "I want you right here on the floor. We can break it in like we did the counters at lunch."

"We're going to break each other if you don't stop that. And how are you going to get this place finished if you're forever sending your help away?" She backed up, then stood up. "I mean it, Dylan. It's daylight."

That stopped him. He looked out the windows. He'd decided before she came into his life that they didn't need curtains. Now he could see the necessity of them. He looked back at her.

"It is daylight for sure, but what does that have to do with me wanting you?" She looked around, suddenly shy. It seemed so out of character for her.

"You'd see me." He cocked a brow. "Okay, I know you've seen me naked before, but now it's different. I'm ready for you."

He took a deep breath, and she flushed and stammered on. "I mean, I know that you want me. Before, when you and I had sex on the counter, you snuck up behind me and...and you seduced me. This time I know that you want me and I'm prepared. I think we should wait until dark."

"Why?" She looked away and he wanted to leap into her mind and find out, but he'd promised her that he wouldn't do that…not unless he had to. He was nearly there when she spoke softly.

"Because I know what I look like without my clothes on." She looked up when Khan came in the room. "I have to go."

She took off out of the house and into the yard. Dylan looked at his brother and decided that he needed advice. Maybe not from him, but his wife for sure. He asked where she was.

"She's mad at me again," Khan said.

Dylan didn't ask what he'd done, because neither of them was in a great mood, and that might be all it took for them to get into a brawl in his new dining room. "She is mad because I said she was a tad cranky and maybe she needed to lay down. I was only trying to make her feel better, but she stomped off saying something about men and their brains. I didn't mean anything but that she looked tired."

"You didn't tell her that, did you?" Dylan knew that he had when his brother turned away from him. "Christ, how am I supposed to figure out how to be the best mate in the world when the one man I'm supposed to be able to look up to is a moron?"

"Hey. That isn't right. All I said was she needed to go and have a fucking nap. How the hell was I supposed to know it was going to cause an all-out war?" Just as he lunged for him, their father stepped between them. "Dad, this is between Dylan and me. I think you should stay out of the way."

"Women problems, right?" Dylan nodded. "Thought so. Well, boys, I'm going to give you the best advice a father can pass to his sons. It's sound and has worked for me for nearly twenty-five years."

"Dad, you've been married for forty." Khan looked at his dad and then at his mom when she stepped in the room as well.

"Right you are, but it took me nearly fifteen to learn what I'm about to tell you." His dad sat down, and Dylan was ready to take notes. His parents had been happy together since he was a kid. He'd never seen them fight, never seen them to be anything but a loving, wonderfully happy couple. Dylan leaned forward when his dad did.

"Shut up." Dylan started to tell him that they'd not spoken when his dad continued. "Just shut up. I don't care if she wants your honest opinion of something or if she's asking you if you like her new recipe. Shut up. It'll settle things in a heartbeat."

"You old fool." His mom came all the way into the room. "What is wrong with you telling them that? You'll have their mates coming to me asking me why I raised such an idiot. Shut up indeed. I should have taken out your tongue with advice like that." She looked at the two of them. "You have to listen. We women know you guys are trying, but there are times when we don't even know what it is we want. So you just have to listen. Try listening to us with your hearts, not your empty heads."

Dylan watched his parents argue and looked at Khan when they stepped out of the room. When Khan got back to work on the floor, so did Dylan. They had about a half dozen more pieces to lay when Khan suddenly sat back.

"Who do we listen to? The man who says that's what he does, or the woman who tells us to listen to our hearts?" Khan looked at the floor. "Why are we doing this when both our mates are pissed at us?"

"Mine isn't pissed. She's embarrassed for me to see her naked." Khan smiled. "What? You think you can help me?"

"Yeah. Monica is mad because I said she needed a nap and I wouldn't go lay down with her. She seems to think that I don't think she's sexy while she's pregnant. Honestly, I'm terrified of hurting her. I mean, look at me compared to her. I'm like an ox and her this little…little flower of a thing. What if I rolled over on her or the baby?"

Khan sounded so horrified that Dylan laughed. "You should tell her that. I mean just like that. You sound that afraid of her and she'll melt."

"You think?" Dylan nodded. "Okay, your problem. You know how Monica was hurt by that prick? Well, she was embarrassed about the scar he'd left her. I took her to bed and kissed every place she had on her until we were…. It worked. She felt better about them because I didn't care."

Dylan looked at the room. They were so close. He grinned at his brother and picked up another slat. He pounded the piece in and Khan hit it with two nails while they each were in thought.

"You know that if we finish this today, we can take our mates somewhere for the entire day? We can go to DC and bug the shit out of Walker and spoil the baby, too." Khan stopped working and grinned.

"And we can take Mom and Dad with us. You know how much they love seeing Baby George." It was evil. Pure and simple, but he loved it and told Khan that.

In less than an hour, they had the floor finished, then another two to clean up the dust and put the things away. Khan even helped him move the two corner cabinets into place and anchor them. By six-thirty, they were both off to find their other halves, and Dylan had a plan.

He was going to show Jack how much he loved her body.

Chapter Eight

Jack walked along the trees and tried not to think about how stupid she felt about her conversation with Dylan. She leaned down to pick up a stick and toss it when something sounded behind her. She turned, thinking it was Dylan. Behind her stood a tiger…a big, fucking white Bengal tiger.

"Nice kitty." The tiger sat and looked at her. "Are you real or are you a were? I guess that would be weretiger. Are you one of those?"

He didn't move. She started back toward the house, but when she took just one step, he stood up as well. When she took a step back, so did he. Jack was afraid to run, because she remembered what Corrine had told her about cats liking to chase, and Jack didn't doubt that this one would run her down and have her for dinner. When he looked to his left, she looked in that direction as well.

"He wants to know where your mate is." Jack looked from Monica to the tiger. "He said that they were supposed to make sure that he had a few hours on his own, and that you're too tasty-looking to let go now. I think he's kidding."

"You *think* he is?" Monica laughed. She stopped by a tree and held onto it for several seconds before she moved toward her.

"I'm lost and a little disorientated. I think he's been chasing me." Jack looked at the tiger. "Not him. There was this wolf here earlier, and I think he was chasing me."

"Monica, what's wrong?" When she sat down hard and looked to be in pain, a great deal of it, she knew. "Are you in labor? Holy shit, woman, what the fuck are you doing out in the middle of the fucking woods in labor?"

The tiger came toward them. She looked at Monica and knew that it wasn't just labor, but the hard stuff. When she put her hand on her belly, she felt the tightening about the same time that she started pushing. Mother fuck. Jack looked at the tiger.

"Can you understand me?" He nodded. "Go to the fucking house and get Khan. He's at my house, Dylan's house. Go there and make them…can they understand you like she does?" He took off.

"Jack. I think they're coming. I think—" She screamed and held onto Jack's hand. "Help me. You have to help me."

"Yeah. I can do this. I had to take a class." She helped her lay down on the ground and took off her pants. There was blood, but not a great deal of it. Jack looked up at Monica and smiled.

"How hard can this be, right?" The next scream had Jack wondering if she was religious enough. The third had her doubting the class, her ability as a woman to handle this, and her sanity at even trying it. Ten minutes later, she was holding the new baby in her hands.

The first panther came over the small hill a few minutes later, the tiger and the rest of them seconds after that. Monica bore down hard, and when Khan shifted in front of her, Jack handed him his son.

"Here, make yourself useful." She knew the baby was all right and that the kid had nothing on his mother when it came to screaming. The next baby, a beautiful little girl, came about the time the rest of them shifted and were pulling on clothes.

She looked at Dylan as she helped Corrine clean up Monica. She couldn't tell if he was mad or not, and right now she was feeling too good to care. Then she noticed that Khan was naked.

"Damn it, Khan, would you please put something over that thing? Somebody might get hurt." She heard him chuckle, then a shuffle of clothes, and knew he was getting dressed. Jack decided she was going to neuter him sometime soon. "See if I help you out again when your wife is running around the woods in labor."

He pulled her up off the ground and into his arms. He hugged her so tightly she was sure that bones would need mending. But it felt good, too. When she wrapped her arms around him, too, he looked down at her.

"You saved them. My family, you saved them for me." He kissed her forehead and stepped back when someone growled. "I owe you more than I'll ever be able to repay. Thank you very much, Jack Bowen."

"I gotta know." She pulled away from Khan and brushed at the tears, and looked at Marc as he continued. "I have to know where the name Jack came from. You are so not a Jack."

"You dork, I haven't always looked like this." He flushed, and she felt bad so she told him. "I was born on the streets. My mother had been a druggie and had died while in labor with me. Two bums, Jack Morton and Duke Crosby, found her body and realized I was still alive…as drugged as my mother, but alive. While Jack had been sober, he'd been a doctor. Duke was just a man who I guess liked to get drunk with his box buddy. When they realized that I was going to be more trouble than I was worth, they took me to the hospital.

When the nurse asked them if I had a name, neither man wanted to have anything to do with 'the man'…what they called the government…and what he might bring down on them. So they named me for both of them. Jack Crosby. Years later, I came across Jack, and he told me the story. Duke had been killed when someone had wanted his box and he wasn't willing to give it up."

Marc nodded. "You know that's the…well, that's the stupidest story I've ever heard. Is any of that true?"

She nodded. "Yes. Every bit of it. The kids at the orphanage made fun of me all the time. And when I was in college, it was very difficult to sign up for classes. It's the reason I ended up working for Kirby Mann."

Jack looked at Dylan. He came toward her as all the pieces fell into place…everything; the house, the pool, and the man she worked for. She didn't realize she'd been sat down with her head between her knees until someone said that she was to stay there. She struggled enough that she was finally set free.

"I need to talk to Caitlynne. She has to know what Mann is doing." She looked over at a man she'd yet to meet yet knew. "Is that the president?"

"Yes. He was also the tiger. He told me that you were a pushy thing and he'd like to hire you." She nodded and looked up at Dylan. "What?"

"I thought I worked for him." She nodded to Caitlynne as she pulled up in front of them in a large SUV. "And her. I knew who she was, but didn't make the connection until just now. She's going to have me put in prison if what I thought was true isn't."

"She won't. She knows there's something going on, and until now, she's not had anything to get things all lined up." Dylan kneeled down in front of her. "I was coming out here to find you and seduce you. I had this idea that I could make you scream out a climax and a promise. One that said you wouldn't be ashamed of your body again."

She nodded and looked at the president as he talked and joked with Khan as he put his wife in the vehicle. When he looked at her, the president nodded, and she nodded back. She wondered what she'd just agreed to, and asked Dylan.

"He can hear us. Everyone here can. As a cat, our hearing is very good. We can hear most any whisper. He knows you're upset, baby, and he understands that you might have been caught in the middle of something."

"I was...I am. Mann is looking for me. I didn't know who before, and now that I do, I'm more afraid for your family. He won't stop. Not with what I know." She wondered if Casey was still safe, and hoped so. "I've done so many things in the name of the covert company I worked for. So many horrible, horrible things. Things I don't even know if I can forgive myself for."

They got into the truck that Reed had driven over. Khan was so happy that he kept pulling her into his arms and hugging her. The fourth or fifth time he came toward her, she told him if he didn't behave she was going to knock him on his ass. He laughed and hugged her, anyway. The man was sappy, that's all there was to it.

An hour later she was sitting in a room with Marshall, Caitlynne, and the president, who'd asked her to call him Warren. She declined. And Dylan was there, as well. He was there because he threatened to simply listen in and tell everyone in the room with him what was being discussed. She was never so happy to have him near her in her life.

~~~

"I started working for the agency right out of college. I had a degree in criminal science, but it wasn't going to do me much good because I had a record." She looked at Caitlynne when she asked her for what. "Grand larceny. I stole a car. I was fifteen and thought that I could sell it and use the money to eat on for a while. I had no idea that the car was worthless; and worst yet, it belonged to a cop, Richard Davenport. He was restoring it."

"Did he have you arrested?" Marshall asked. She smiled at him. "Or did he just have you given community service and put you into some home?"

"Yes, he had me arrested. But he and his wife also took me in. I spent the next four years living with them and going straight. They helped me get into college and made me save my money. He also taught me to trust no one. He saved my life a great many times with that bit of sage advice."

Marshall nodded. "You went to work for Kirby Mann. What was the—?"

"I didn't work for Mann until later. The first man I worked for was Conrad Garrett. He got promoted right after I joined the team. I think he's dead, though."

"Yes, he killed himself about a year or so ago." Caitlynne looked down at something on the desk. "Tell me who else is on the team."

"There are about fifty-three of us. Two of them are now dead as of the night I ended up at the Clements's house. I killed them both when they fired at me. Would you like to see their files?" Caitlynne looked at the president. "If I'm going to go before a firing squad, I might as well make it worth my while."

"You have them on you?" She stood up and went to the front of the house. Dylan went with her. She went to the first step and pulled it up. It was still where she'd left it. Going back to the study, she handed the thumb drive to her.

Caitlynne in turn handed it to Reed, who'd been asked to join them when she said it was on a drive.

"The files are marked, and you should be able to figure them out." She went to the computer with Reed and stood behind him, pointing them out as she explained. "This is the names and complete files of each member of the group. Mine is there as well, but little of the information is correct. I didn't alter it. I just never gave up the right information."

Reed closed that one and opened the next. He stared at if for several seconds before he looked around the room. He didn't say anything when she told him to open the first file.

"These are files that were in Garrett's office before he left. I had been in the office for…I was there, and the file was there, so I took it. I did return it later, but all the pictures were gone. I have the originals." Warren asked Reed what they were.

"They're pictures of you, sir. You and Marshall." Warren looked at her. "They're pictures of the two of you in bed. Why would he want these?"

"Because he thought he could blackmail him." Jack pointed to the next folder. "This was his plan. I don't think it would have done him a great deal of good without the rest, so I guess he abandoned the idea."

"And the tapes? Where are they? With you, too?" She shook her head. "Do you plan to use them, as well?"

"No. They're in your private home in the Hamptons. They've been there all along. There's a swing in the yard. Under the left leg is a box. Those as well as the letters are stored there."

She leaned over Reed, hurt more than she thought she'd be. "This is the records of all our assignments. I updated them when I could. Also, you'll find a record of all the chips we had implanted into us. I had mine—"

"Jack, look at me." She stretched her neck but continued going over the things on the computer, ignoring Warren. "I asked you to look at me. You may not have worked for me before but you do now, and I want you to respect my requests."

She stood. "It was no more a request than when Corrine asked George to take out the trash. I don't trust people, that's a given. But I'd never do anything...knowingly do anything to harm the man that I assumed I worked for."

"I know that now. And I wanted to thank you. You have no idea what those would have done to our families had they gotten out. No one must know."

She decided to tell it all. "Everyone knows, sir. The only people who might not know are the hobos on the street, and only if they haven't seen the two of you together. The entire country knows you and Marshall are lovers. If you guys let it out there, it's doubtful that anyone would care." He started to speak. "I have the floor, thanks, so just shut up and listen. You mark my words. No one gives two shits who you sleep with, so long as the economy keeps on the way it is."

"But Garrett thought they would. Why else would he have taken those pictures and set us up? He thought that the country would care."

"He thought that everyone would care, because he was stupid. That man might have run a good game for a while, but he was the stupidest man I ever met." She pointed to the computer. "Do you know that there are so many memos on this thing that never got sent because the man couldn't string two words together and make it work?"

Marshall laughed. Jack leaned back over the computer to continue from there when Caitlynne asked her about Snow. Jack stood there for several seconds before she moved to her chair again.

"She's safe. I spoke to her a few days ago. She's not happy with me, but she's safe." Jack turned to the people in the room. "She had nothing to do with anything but helping me remove the chip from my head. I'd been overseas on assignment, and when I returned, I'd bumped my head on an open cabinet door. She was in her office when I asked her to look at it and to stitch it up if it needed it. She pulled it out, and I knew something was wrong."

"You had the chip on you when you came here. It was broken, but Reed helped us figure it out. How do you think Mann found out you'd had it removed?"

"He knew right after I came back from Europe. I was to come in for a physical, and I figured they'd plant another one in me or had figured out that I knew. Casey said that the x-rays that she took of me looking for another one probably set the sucker off. She said if they ever wanted me to come in and have a little operation, I was to get her out of town. When Mann started harping on me about the yearly physical three months too early, I sent her away."

"Where is she?" Marshall asked. Jack shook her head at the question. "We can bring her here, keep her safe," Marshall insisted. "There's no reason for her to be unhappy when we can help her."

"Yeah, well, I thought I was safe, too, until I went to scope out the house I was supposed to target. They'd been there all day waiting, taking care of everything, so when I got there, all they had to do was pop a couple in my head and make an anonymous call." She looked at Dylan to finish. "I wasn't doing too bad at first. Once I jumped over the fence, I went to the doghouse on the neighbor's property. I'd already stashed my street clothes there and a set of night ones. Black on black to hide better. I was bleeding pretty well by then, and my head was pounding. But I knew hanging around would get me killed."

"Do you know what time you were hit?"

She nodded. "21:57."

"That means you were off line for twelve hours before Dylan found you. Where did you go?"

"I don't know for sure. I had to backtrack until I got so lost that I didn't know how to get back. I had planted a car as a means to escape, but I couldn't remember how to get to it. Then there was the blood. I couldn't keep walking around leaving a path of breadcrumbs for them, so I found an empty building and stayed there long enough to rest. The next thing I knew, I was seeing this house in the clearing and had to get rid of the drive. I couldn't go far, I knew, so I put it under the broken step."

"And had you not survived, how would you have been justified for all this work?" Jack didn't answer, but Marshall knew. "Casey has a copy, or knows where one is."

They stared at one another, and she just knew that he was searching her mind. She had no idea if he could actually do that, but figured if Dylan could, then it could stand to reason that everyone could. She felt a small touch, a sort of tickle to her mind, and stilled.

"He can't read your mind. But you should know that you and I can speak this way and no one else can hear us." She glanced at him. *"All mates have a link. I would imagine that Warren and Marshall have one, as well, though I don't know of any other gay weres, but I'm sure there are plenty."*

"This thing, this link, is it just weres or can anyone do it? The reason I ask is because when I found Monica, she said a wolf was chasing her and she was a little off. Could someone have gone in and fucked with her mind?" Dylan stood suddenly and left the room. *"Dylan?"*

"I'll be right back. Help them as much as you can, but don't mention the wolf yet. I want to check on something." She looked at the others in the room and smiled.

"Casey doesn't know what it is, but she knows where to find it. And I've set it up that if anything should happen to her, anything, the file hits the papers." Marshall nodded. "I trust her because she's trusted me. You? I don't know."

"Understandable. But if someone else were to get the file from her, what then? Do you know what that can do to National Security?" Marshall got up to pace. "Even if we take out the pictures of Warren and me, the other stuff in there would destroy all we've worked for."

"I never said it was a file." Reed looked at her, and she smiled at him. "I know probably more about computers and programs than four of him. He's good, but I'm better. Casey checks in weekly. She misses one week its fine, two it notifies me. If I don't respond within a week, it hits the papers, all of them."

Marshall sat down next to Warren and reached for his hand. "You know she hasn't contacted you. You know she's still alive."

"I spoke with her yesterday. She wants to come home but knows that if she does she's dead. She also knows that I'd been hurt. Hard not to pick up a paper and see my face plastered all over the place. But what she doesn't know about is what you people are. She is a great friend and a better doctor. If you ever needed another doctor, she would be the person I'd call."

The door opened behind them, and Dylan filled the space. He was upset, and she went to him. When he kissed her, she could feel the coiled tension in his body. He looked at the people assembled there.

"Someone knows Jack is here. A wolf came onto the property today and found Monica out in the woods. He read her mind and was clumsy about it. He left his print behind, and I've been able to see what he found." He looked at her. "Mann knows where you are."

Chapter Nine

Kirby moved around the room without touching anything, and when he did touch something, he was careful to wipe his prints away. He had been hiding there for a whole day, and he was already going stir crazy. He just hoped to fuck that the books he'd read were right, and that without taking his blood the vampire couldn't find him.

His wife was dead, as was his daughter. He knew the moment that he'd gotten the call from Lucius that he would kill them. The man did not strike him as a houseguest sort of person. And his family had been spoiled. He knew this as he'd done it to them. When things did not go their way or they didn't get what they wanted, they tended to whine about it. It was one of the reasons he gave in, and also the reason he worked late several times a week and went in on most weekends. He loved them, but he had made it hard for himself. And Lucius did not strike him as a patient man. Then there was the blood that had been on Lucius's jacket.

Kirby still couldn't believe that he'd seen it or that he'd done what he had. When Lucius had sent him out of the room to speak to…or kill the wolf, Kirby had gone to the bedroom and found the coat there. He'd not even remembered him having one on, but that was beside the point. But the blood had been there, and he'd taken a sample. Actually, he'd taken several samples. He'd had them tested the very next day to see who or what he might have killed.

Three of them came back as canine. Kirby had no idea whether it was actual dog or a werewolf like the one he'd had as a guest. But two of them were his wife and daughter. The blood splatter of all the samples had been enough to convince him that they'd been murdered, as all the blood samples he'd taken had been. So Kirby had run.

He didn't go near the window, nor did he order in at his new place. It was not the worst he could have moved into on a temporary basis, but it was as close to slum-like that he'd ever been in. Kirby hadn't worked for one of the largest agencies in the world to not know a thing or two about keeping yourself safe. He'd even put on a disguise to hide who he was to the taxi drivers, as well as when he'd gone into Walmart to get the things he'd need. In each instance, after he'd had to talk to or ask for services from someone, he'd changed his appearance. He was quite proud of himself about it, too.

He'd gone to the store before coming here and had purchased a small microwave and enough shelf-life foods that required no refrigeration that he could live for nearly a month. He'd also picked up a cheap laptop. The bottled water sat in a cooler that he'd brought, too. His clothes, packed for such an occasion, had been updated and freshened every few months or so. He had even made sure that his pictures on his IDs were updated to the current year, as well as his aging face.

He had paid cash for the room and had paid for the week. Knowing that someday he'd have to leave in a hurry and not be found, he'd had several IDs made for himself and his family, and money enough that they would be able to start over if need be. He had never dreamed he'd be doing this on his own. Sitting down again, he pulled out the only thing he'd taken from the house other than the things from the garage storage…a picture of them all together at Christmas. He sobbed again at their loss.

Putting the picture into the large case, he glanced at the contents. He was glad now that he'd been able to put this away without his family knowing. Lucky, too, that he'd been able to be in on the ground floor of the mess that had gotten Small arrested and eventually led to Garrett's suicide.

No one knew that he'd been watching over the books and sending the money to each of their offshore accounts for them. He'd been paid well, very well, but he still took a percentage of their deposits as well. He'd amassed well over twenty million in a very short amount of time, and was thrilled that he'd never used his own name when dealing with them. The others had gone down because they were careless and stupid.

Kirby's money had never seen the inside of a bank other than to transfer it to cash, and had never left the garage once he put it in there. It was his run money and nothing more. Setting up a dummy account with one of his aliases and a business that did nothing more than take up space, he would deposit the money directly into the account, then write checks to another dummy corporation and cash them. He even filed a tax form every year and paid his taxes on that money like a good boy.

Looking at the computer that sat on the table, he wondered again if he was doing the right thing. Giving up just about all he knew was going to make his life on the run a little more difficult, but he had to try and appease some of what he'd done to his wife by saying yes all those years ago. She deserved better than whatever Lucius had done to her and his child.

Kirby walked over to the computer again and sat in front of it. It was all there. Files, names, dates, anything and everything he needed to expose not only Lucius, but everyone else in the organization, as well. He'd even put in information about Small and the things he'd been able to dig up about him over the past several months. He'd had no use for it when the man had ended up in prison, but Kirby had held onto it. He thought someday he might write a book...inder a pen name, of course. But the one person he had nothing on was that fucking woman.

Crosby had been nothing but exemplary from birth to now. The one thing that had been on her record had been expunged years ago when Davenport had gone to the courts on her behalf and had it removed. The judge had taken one look at her life after the jail time and had it done. Kirby had never told her about it. He'd let her think that he'd been magnanimous by letting her work for him. Fat lot of good that had been for him...she'd still fucked him over.

Crosby had done each job he'd assigned her, and though she killed for him, that didn't make her guilty. It simply made her a perfect employee. He'd had a chance to look over her record, too. Crosby had never been caught with anything. Going in and out of the building, she'd been checked thoroughly. But he knew as surely as he was looking at his own stolen files that she'd gotten some out, if not everything. She was that fucking good.

He hoped to Christ that wherever her body was—and he was pretty sure she was dead now—that no one found anything on it that he'd not taken out of his files he was sending to Bowen the Bitch. Smiling, he looked at the file he'd created to give to the Feds. There was enough stuff in it to put him away forever if he were to get caught, but there was enough information in the deleted file that would get him shot. Kirby had not been a very good man. Not now, and certainly not in his youth. He'd murdered to get where he'd been, and he knew that he'd do it again if he had to.

He glanced up at the television and saw his nemesis, Caitlynne Bowen...Bowen the Bitch in the flesh. There was another woman he could have gone his entire life without knowing. She was bossy and a know it all. Of course, she was his boss, but that didn't mean that he had to like the way she lorded herself over him. Or the way she made him come to her office to go over the slightest entries in his bookkeeping. He'd been able to do whatever he liked with Garrett. Where did that fucking cunt get off telling him he needed to curb his spending? He turned the TV up to see what she was doing now.

"...no longer considered a threat to National Security. Her name has been cleared of all charges concerning the death of Vern and Cindy Clements and Ruby, their daughter. If anyone knows of Agent Jack Crosby's whereabouts, please tell her that she is not wanted, but we still need to speak to her. If you are listening to this, agent, we would like to offer you a safe haven until all this is cleared up and we find the person or persons responsible for the murders. Again, Agent Jack Crosby is no longer wanted in questioning for the murders of the Clements family. We are currently looking into other information that has come to light in recent days. It not only shows that Agent Crosby is not guilty of the crimes charged against her, but also indicates that she had information about who the actual murderers were. We'll have more details as we verify them. Thank you." She walked off the podium rather than answer any questions. The fucking cunt.

Kirby turned it off. He sat there for several minutes with nothing going through his head but one thought. She knew.

Bowen knew something. He got up to pull a bottle of water from the cooler and put it back. He reached in and pulled out the bottle of tequila that he'd stashed in there, as well.

Pouring himself a healthy drink in one of the plastic water glasses, he thought of his boss. Bowen the Bitch, as he'd taken to calling her early in her career as his boss, wouldn't put anything out there unless she was positive about it. She was a ball buster for sure, but she also knew her job. But she didn't have Crosby. Or so she said.

He wondered if she was there, put into the big house of Bowen's so that no one could find her, and she was singing all sorts of shit. It would be like the two of them to get together and try to bring him down. He glanced at the email addressed to Bowen the Bitch and realized that now, if she did have Crosby or not, it was useless to him as a way to save some face. Crosby had already given it all to her.

He poured himself another glassful after drinking the first one down. After deleting the email, he started a new one. This one he was sending as soon as he was finished with it. No more dicking around. He was going to walk away from this shit with a clear mind and a cleaner slate. Kirby wrote until he couldn't see the keys, then finished off the other half a bottle of the tequila and crawled into the lumpy bed. He would rest a few hours, then get up and do it again until he was finished.

~~~

"What do you mean he isn't at his home? Did you go to the correct address?" The wolf nodded. "Let me see it."

Timmy Huston handed him the paper that Lucius had given him three days ago. It was the right address. He looked at the wolf, which was still in a supine position on the floor when he gave Lucius the paper but quickly looked back now, knowing which of them was the inferior.

"Did you go inside the house?" Lucius asked.

Timmy nodded, keeping his head down.

"What did you find? Maybe he simply went out for a cup of sugar from the neighbor's house."

"I watched it for two days before coming here. I even tried to track him. His scent went to the garage, where he pulled something from the floor. Then he walked back to the house. I caught his scent out to the front sidewalk, then nothing. He might have taken a cab or gotten a ride. I couldn't follow it because of the many cars on his street."

Lucius kicked him. When the wolf shifted and landed on his feet after hitting the wall, Lucius hoped that he'd try and attack him, but he only stayed where he was. But now he was upright and not in a subservient position. Lucius thought about killing him but was leery of the wolf. He'd survived the kick, so Lucius knew killing him might not be easy.

"You'll find him or I'll kill you." The wolf snarled in response. "If you think that frightens me, you're stupider than your predecessor. And he was an idiot."

Lucius watched him pace. He wished now, like he did with the human, that he'd taken his blood. He'd had the wife's and thought that that had been enough, but now he knew it hadn't been. He also had a feeling that the human knew that he'd killed his wife and child. He'd not meant to, but their excessive whining and crying had driven him over the edge.

The trial was in five days. Just five days for everything to go away so that he could get Small into the White House. He knew that the man had confessed. He'd even read it…but the man was going to get him what he wanted, and that was war.

War was so wonderfully filling for his kind. People could disappear from a field of combat and never be missed. He and others like him had been so plentiful because of the ability to turn so many without fear of being caught.

He smiled after the wolf left, thinking about the many children he'd created and left. He and others of his kind hadn't even bothered to train them, knowing that they would be dead within a month or so. Some would have survived, and those were the ones that he called to him when he needed something done. They were the killers, the ones that would do anything to anyone to get what they wanted. The strong.

He knew Small was an idiot and a fool. But he knew that he could control him, because he was greedy and only looked out for himself. He'd promise him anything and everything for his help. He would tell him that he would live forever. Lucius knew that he'd be dead once the last of the information he wanted was in his hands.

Small would never be president or even a janitor in the building again, or anywhere for that matter, but he would get into the one place that Lucius could not. Because he'd been inside of it, he would know the building as well as his own, and that was what Lucius was counting on. Counting on him knowing where the secret entrances were, and how to get around the guards. The man had been a thief to his country; he had to know a great deal.

Someone, many years ago, had put a spell on the building. The very foundation and bricks had been protected by a powerful wizard, and now no one of his kind could enter, not even with permission. And it was Lucius's fault.

Lucius supposed that he shouldn't have pissed the man off. But he'd been talking about his plan, telling anyone that would listen to him what he was going to do once he made that stupid man cause a war of all wars.

"You would actually create war?" Lucius had nodded, drunk off the blood of a wolf he'd just had. "You would feed off the dead like an animal?"

"No. We cannot feed off the dead. The blood must be fresh, the heart still beating. We would collect those, the ones that lay dying in the fields, and drink from them. The feast would be plentiful." He had closed his eyes in appreciative bliss. "They would be dying, anyway. What difference would it make to them?"

"And what if you change one? What of that man's family then? Would you not feel remorse when he could not be given a proper burial? Would you even care how his family felt if they were to find out?" The man, his name no longer in his mind, had shaken his head. "You are not a man, but a monster."

"I am both, actually. A man who would like nothing more than to live the rest of his lifetimes as a monster." He'd let his fangs drop to try and impress on the wizard that he was big and powerful, but he didn't seem to care at all.

"You're a monster, all right, but nothing more." The man shifted in his seat, settling down for the full details, as Lucius remembered. "And how do you plan to carry this out? You do have a plan, do you not?"

He'd told him. All of it. He was going to enter the White House and murder all those within. A grand plan, he realized now, because of the overwhelming amount of people in the place, but back then not so many as now.

"I will turn them all and have them creatures of the night with me. They shall be my minions and me their master. They will protect me when I rest. I will—"

"If they are creatures such as yourself, how will they protect you when you rest? Won't they have to rest, as well? I mean, who will protect any of you if all of you are down for the day?" This had been the first of many questions the man had that Lucius had had no answer for, and after a while he knew that he'd have to rethink his plan and make it perfect. He realized that this one was full of holes.

"This is merely a plan, not the actual execution of it. There are going to be flaws in it. There are for every plan that one makes." The man nodded. "Have you ever gone to do something and realize right away you have forgotten some vital ingredient or something important, and had to return at a later time to complete it?"

"No. When I go to do something, I do it right the first time. Then, unlike you, I don't have to go back and do it over and over to get it right." He stood up. "You let me know when you have it perfect. When you do, I'll listen to you prattle on again."

So, years later, he'd found the man again and told him of his perfected plan. The man sat there for the entire time and hadn't done anything more than nod and smile a few times. After he was finished, Lucius asked him what he'd thought. The wizard smiled and told him what he'd done, as well.

"I have been able to go into the building myself. A nice piece of craftsmanship, if I do say so myself. They let you have a free tour of it if you want, and I did. Had to see how your plan was going to go from the planning stage to the execution part. Gotta tell you, had you been able to pull it off before I got in, you might have been able to do just what you said."

Lucius nodded, then frowned. "Had I? What do you mean had I gotten in before you? I will still be able to get in, and you know that this plan is perfect."

"It is. It was. But now it's not. I fixed it." Lucius started to ask him how, but he told him anyway. "I'm a pretty good wizard, as you know, and unlike you, I'm always prepared. So I went to the big house and did a little magic on the place, so neither you nor your kind can enter."

"You can't do that." The man nodded and smiled bigger. "Well, I will just have someone invite me in. I'll get in that way. I'll...why do you shake your head?"

"Thought of that, too. Can't enter, ever. Not anyone of your kind. I also made it so that if you do try, or any vampire tries to enter, they'll go up into dust before they step foot on the first step to the place."

Lucius had roared his anger. The wizard hadn't moved. When he grabbed him around the neck, his fingers burned, and it felt as if a dagger of silver had been stabbed into his hand. He dropped him immediately to nurse his injuries in a corner of the bar. The wizard moved to stand over him.

"You can't harm another wizard, either. Not you or any of your children. You cannot, nor can they control anyone that would harm a wizard of any kind even if they are causing you harm. You have messed with the wrong one." He stood up, then leaned down and touched his forehead with his thumb before standing again. "You are marked to us. Any wizard will know who you are and what you've done to one of my kind." Then he simply walked away.

But there was a way in. Small was the key. And once he was inside, he was going to have Small give him whatever information he had at his fingertips. Then Lucius was going to give it all to the highest bidder and sit back and wait for the bloodbath. Lucius rubbed his hands together in anticipation. He would be the greatest vampire ever born. Or in his case, made. Lucius made his way to the sublevels of his home. He needed to rest, then to plan. The trial could not go on. He needed Small.

Chapter Ten

Dylan watched the news with Jack and the rest of his family. Caitlynne had let them read over what she was going to say, and everyone had approved and thought it was a good idea. Everyone but Jack. She'd been staring off into space like she was now since after her meeting in the study.

"I thought that tomorrow we'd go to the falls at the back of my property and have a picnic. We could stay all day if you want." She nodded, and he knew she wasn't really paying attention. "I could strip you down and make love to you in the water. It's probably very warm right now."

"That'll be nice." She looked at him. "They're going to have me put into prison, aren't they? I know they said they weren't, but I killed a shit ton of people for Mann, and I'm pretty sure that no matter how you dress it up, I still pulled the trigger."

"Caitlynne told you that you were a victim, like the people you killed. And according to the list you provided, not one person on that list was exactly what she'd consider model citizens." He took her hand when she stood up. "Jack, come away with me for a few hours and let's forget this."

She told him she would go, but she wanted to get something from their room. He went to the kitchen to throw together some of the things that he'd bought yesterday for their picnic. When she came down, he could see that she'd armed herself, of which he had no problem. It was the sadness in her eyes that bothered him.

He pulled her into his arms. "It's going to be all right, baby. You'll see. Mann will turn himself in, or some agent will pop a camp in his head." He'd hoped that she'd laugh, and she did.

"Its pop a cap, not camp, and being a fifth grade teacher, I would think you'd have heard that term a great deal." She kissed him on the neck. "Let's go and lose ourselves today, okay? I don't even want to think about what we have and what we know."

"Agreed." Lifting the basket, she eyed him. "I have nothing in this basket but things to sooth my lovely mate. If a few things that we might need got in here, we'll just have to make the best of the situation. And I don't know about you, but I will be glad when we can have our home back. All this company is driving me nuts." They went out to his garage, and he settled himself over his bike. She looked at him with a cocked brow.

He handed her a helmet. "I thought we were going to walk. Isn't that the best way to get around back there?"

"It is if you don't know the terrain like I do. Hop on." He waited for her to wrap her arms and legs around him before he started the bike. Her heat wrapped around him, distracting him, but he had plans today, which included being between her hot thighs. He took off with her laughter ringing in his ears.

He took her around the outer edges of the property, the long way around to where he wanted them to end up. Stopping twice to stretch, he showed her where he knew that some deer played. They had also stopped to watch a hawk mate with his female in the air. By the time they got to the falls, her cheeks were pink and they were both starving.

"You were maybe feeding an army," she teased him as she took out the containers. "I see we have cold chicken…my favorite, by the way. And macaroni salad and potato. One, two, three…five ham sandwiches on rye, and dill pickles."

He reached in to the basket when she opened a pickle and chomped on it. "I have also, for the lady, some cheese cake bites, as well as strawberries and cream. Iced tea, as well as some very lovely white wine, if you so desire."

They sat on the blanket he'd brought and filled their plates. While she put salads on his and hers, he opened the wine and poured them both a glass. Dylan laughed when he saw the portion of chicken she'd put on her plate.

"Hungry?" She smiled at him as she ate a leg. "I hope you know that I didn't just bring you out here for the food and view. I plan to ravage you later."

"I know. That's why I'm storing up energy." She handed him one of the pieces on her plate. "You should know that you'd better be ready for me, too. I've been very lonely of late."

His body tensed, and he growled low. He suddenly didn't want to waste time on eating when he had her in front of him. When she put out her hand to stop him from moving toward her, he stopped.

"I'm really hungry. I mean it. If you make me miss my meal, I'm going to be very pissy with you." She looked up at the sky, and he knew now why she'd lingered over a flower, and had wanted to see the den he'd found better. She was waiting for dark. Dylan took her plate away from her.

"The food can wait. I can't." She moved back and looked panicky. "I'm going to make love to you with the sun shining over us. I'm going to touch you in ways you can't imagine."

"Dylan, I told you. I'm not comfortable with you seeing me naked. Please." He shook his head, grabbed her leg, and brought her to him. "Dylan."

Her shoes came off first. He tossed them away from them, but not so far that they wouldn't be able to find them. Then he slid his hands up her thighs and over her smooth skin.

"When I shaved your legs I had never enjoyed touching anything as much as I did you. Your skin was so soft and smooth. Hearing your soft moans made my cock hurt, but I couldn't stop until I was finished." Dylan pulled her to him so that she was on his lap, facing him. "I want to touch you again, feel your warmth in my hands."

Her shirt pulled up over her head, and he did that now. Her bra, a pretty little pink thing, made his mouth water, and he licked along the curve of her breasts that was exposed. Her moan made him want more. Unhooking the front clasp, he opened the cups slowly and watched her full breasts spill into his hands. Leaning down, he kissed the first of many scars he knew she had.

"Tell me how you got this one." He licked along the entire length of it, knowing it was from a knife. "How badly were you hurt when this was done?"

"I was in training. I took a step to the right instead of the left and he grazed me. I got seven stitches and a write up for being stupid." He nodded and moved to the other breast and another scar, where he asked her the same question. "Bullet. I was going into a market while it was being robbed. I took exception to that, because I love that little shop and the people who own it."

"Did you kill him?" She nodded. "Good. Where did you get this one and this one? They look to be from about the same time."

They were along her ribs. He held her softly and kissed each one of them, then took her nipple into his mouth for a small taste. Her breath caught, and he looked up at her.

"I was...I was supposed to take out a target and.... Dylan, are you going to do this to every scar on me? If you are, then you're going to be a long fucking time before you are inside of me."

"I want you to be able to make love to me in the daylight, with the light on if need be." She wrapped her hands around his neck, and he rolled her to her back. "I want to take you out here someday and take you in the way of my kind. Hard and fast. I want to have you stand against the tree so I can enter you from behind and watch your breasts swing when I fuck you."

She moved from beneath him and stood up. He was sure she was going to bolt, but she looked around the woods and took off her shorts and panties as she moved to the nearest tree. When she was leaned over it, her hands braced against it, she turned to look at him.

"Like this?" She spread her legs wider and looked again. "Or do you prefer this? Come here, Dylan, and show me what you have for me."

He reached into the basket and stood up. He knew she could see what he had in his hand, and he knew she was excited. He began pulling off his clothes as he moved behind her.

"I've wanted to use this on you since I ordered it." Her breathing increased and her scent drove him wild. "Do you have any idea how lovely you look like this? So wet and ready for me?"

Dylan moved the dildo into her sheath slowly. She was so wet it slid in without any problems. He watched her as he danced it in and out of her. When he turned it on, she cried out and moved back against it with each of his strokes.

"I want to drink from you while I play with you. Turn around and back against the tree." He left her standing there so that he could get his shirt and put it on the bark behind her. "I don't want you hurt."

"I'm hurting now. Please, I want you to…please, Dylan." He asked her what she wanted him to do. "I want you to make me come by eating me. Then I want to suck on your cock until you come down my throat."

"I like that plan." He dropped down in front of her and moved the dildo back and forth, not touching her clit. "You're going to come for me, and when you do, I'm going to drink all you offer me."

She nodded, and he moved his mouth to her clit and licked the nubbin. When her knees started to tremble, he held her steady with his hands. Putting the dildo aside for a moment, he spread her open for him and took her with his tongue.

Her juices soaked his chin and dripped down to his chest. He lapped at her over and over as he slid his finger…first one, then a second…into her. She was crying out his name. Now uninhibited, she screamed loudly and often. When she came, he slid a finger into her tight bud and felt her contract around him again. He stood up when her body was still convulsing.

"Suck me." She nodded, dropped down in front of him, wrapped her mouth around him. "Christ."

She was hot, and her tongue moved along him like he was an all-day sucker. Even as he tried to slow her down, he fucked her mouth. Her hands cupped his balls gently, and he felt them tighten. He was so close to coming that when she slid soaking fingers up his ass and pressed deep inside of him, he wrapped his hands in her hair and fucked her hard as he came, crying out her name. She licked him from tip to root while he tried to catch his breath. Finally, he had to beg her to stop.

Dropping to his knees, then pulling her down over him, he held her. Pulling out pieces of bark from her hair, he thought of the danger she was in and pulled her tighter.

"Dylan? Can I tell you something without you freaking out?" He chuckled, and she sat up and looked down at him. "I'm serious."

"Yes. And for the record, I have never freaked out. I am known in my family as the laid-back one." He pulled her back over him. "Tell me. I'm right here for you."

"I love you." He didn't move, afraid that he'd heard her wrong. When she looked at him again, he felt himself tumble into her eyes. She loved him. Rolling her to her back, he stood up and went to the basket. He came back with the small blue box that he'd gotten for her yesterday.

"I was going to make soft and romantic love to you out here and then feed you berries and wine. I had this whole thing planned out where you would be so overwhelmed that you'd say yes without thinking what a dork I am." He took the ring out of the box and held it out so it glistened in the sun. "I love you, too, Jack. I want to spend the rest of my life showing you just how much. Will you marry me?"

"I'm naked." He nodded and winked. "You should know that if this part of your proposal and my acceptance gets in the story when you're ever asked to tell someone how you proposed, I'm going to castrate you."

"Duly noted. Will you say yes so I can make love to you again?" She shook her head, and his heart thudded. "You won't say yes?"

"Oh no, I'm saying yes to that, but I want food before you make love to me. I told you, I'm starved." He slipped the diamond on her finger and kissed her gently. "Let's eat. I'm hungry for you again."

~~~

Jack entered the house and looked at the ring on her finger again. When she'd asked him how he could have gotten her something so huge, he'd told her that he'd done well in the market and had bought up a few properties cheap. He told her that he worked because he loved to, not because he had to. She didn't ask him anything else. Khan was sitting in the kitchen when she entered.

"Don't you have a home?" He stood up slowly, and she knew something was wrong. "What is it? What's happened? Are the babies and Monica all right?"

"They're fine. Everyone is…sit down, Jack." She shook her head. "I'd rather you sat, because when I tell you this, I don't want to have to dodge bullets as I run for my life."

She took the gun from the back of her pants and laid it on the table where he was. Then she reached down to her ankle, took the small one out from there, and put it with the other one. He looked at her after staring at the guns.

"That's all the guns I have on me. You want my knives, you're going to have to take them from me." She crossed her arms over her chest. "Spill it or I will you."

Dylan came in then and stood beside her. He knew, she realized, and turned to him. He didn't look any happier than Khan did. Before she could reach for the gun and shoot one of them, Khan spoke.

"Casey Snow's body was found about an hour ago. They said she'd been murdered and—fuck." She didn't mean to fall forward, but all the blood had rushed from her head and her legs gave out. She ended up sitting, after all, this time with her head between her legs.

"I have to see her body." Neither man answered her, nor would they let her sit up. "It might not be her. I have to—"

"It's her. They identified her with her dental records. Her body was burned, and she—"

"Who?" Jack demanded. Khan looked at Dylan, then at her. "Who was the dentist? I'm sure if you tell me a certain name that it's not her. Tell me, damn it."

"Carl Wilkins." She put her head back between her legs and took several deep breaths before she sat up and looked at them.

"She's in trouble. I have to go to her." She stood up, picked up her guns, and started putting them back on her body. "We had it set up that she would go to the morgue and claim a body. Then she'd have it taken to a funeral home where this guy I know works. He's one of my informants. He's fixed things for me before when I had to get someone safe."

"Where is she?" She turned to Dylan, knowing that he would try and go with her. She couldn't let him. She was shaking her head as she answered him.

"She's here. She never left. Better to hide in plain sight than out in unfamiliar territory. But you can't go with me. She'll spook and run."

"Deal with it. I'm going. If you don't take me, I'll follow you. Either way, I'm there." She looked at Khan, hoping for him to say he'd make his brother stay.

"I'm going, too. We'll go as cats. No one will ever see us." She shook her head again, and Khan grabbed her. "You aren't leaving this house alone."

She sat down and tried to think. She knew that if she left there they'd get killed trying to find her. If she took them, they'd get killed if it was a trap. She looked at them both. It was going to have to be both their ways.

"Can you leap from a moving truck as a cat?" Both nodded. "I know the old saying about cats landing on their feet, but you can't bullshit me. Can you do it?"

"Yes. We can do it. We've done it before. Where are we headed?" She looked at Dylan and smiled. He grinned back.

"To hell and back." She sat them both down and told them what had to happen. Then she let that sink in while she fixed herself a sandwich. She had no idea why she was eating so much lately, but she'd not gained a single pound, either. She was eating it when they looked ready for the rest.

"When I tell you to jump, you'll have to do it then. There is no margin for error, nor can you hesitate. The place you have to go is between a rock and a fast-moving river. Either one will take you away if you don't do this right."

"There's some terrain there that had some large timber on it. Is that still out there, or do you know if it's been sold off? It would make good cover for us when we come in behind you." She shook her head at Dylan's question.

"The timber is still there. I won't sell it off. But there is a house back there. A log cabin that I built when I first got into college. My name isn't on the paper work, but it's still mine." Dylan sat down.

"You outbid me," Dylan said. She looked at him, confused. "You remember, Khan, a few years ago when the property came up for auction? I told you that I was going to get it and you made fun of me for weeks when I didn't. Christ, I wanted that place."

"Well, if anything happens to me, it's yours." She regretted it as soon as she said it. "I'm sorry. I was trying for a joke and failed. Casey had all she would need for years. I had a well dug and hit a gas pocket. It took some wiggling, but I was able to get a lifetime of free gas from it without a name. It's under a corporation, labeled a vacation home."

"And that's where she is?" Khan asked. She nodded. "Then when do we go in and get her?"

She looked around the room. She didn't want to do this. No one but Casey had ever been there before, and she knew that it wasn't up to Dylan's standards. She had built it all on her own, even cutting the timber by herself. It had been the hardest and most fulfilling work of her life, and it had only taken her five years.

"Tonight. We'll leave here at eight. Make sure that you're ready. It's important that we get there before midnight. The alarms are set then."

Chapter Eleven

Khan was getting sick. He'd never been a good rider, and being tossed around in the bed of Dylan's truck wasn't helping. He lay down and glared at his brother. He was sitting there as if he didn't have a care in the world.

"I don't. She said yes, and I'm as happy as I could ever be. And tomorrow we're going to the courthouse to get married." Dylan moved closer to him in an apparent attempt to help him be steady. *"We should be coming up on the area she was talking about, I think. She said to tell you that she will be stopping in a few minutes. She has something to tell you."*

"If this has been a joke I'm going to murder her." Dylan laughed. The truck pulled over deep in the woods, and she opened the door. The light didn't come on, for which Khan was happy. He didn't want to have to let her see how ill he really was. She came around to the back of the bed.

"Dylan said that you'd be able to speak to me if I pledged to you." Khan nodded, suddenly happy she'd done this now. "I want you to know that if this means that you're going to be calling me at all hours of the night for my pancake recipe, then I will revoke it."

Khan moved toward her and licked her face. She smacked him away and looked at Dylan, who had sat down. She looked back at him and into his eyes.

"I pledge to you." The connection was immediate and he licked her again, but pulled back when Dylan growled. This woman had saved his wife and children, and would forever hold a special place in his heart.

"Okay. If there's nothing else like a blood oath or anything, we'll get going. The pass you have to jump at is in less than a half mile. Please make sure you do it precisely when I say to go." Both nodded, and she went back to the truck. When she touched his mind, he wasn't even surprised by her request.

"You have to keep him safe for me. Please, Khan. He's everything to me, like your wife and children are to you." He told her he would. *"And you, too. Monica will kick my ass if I don't bring you back safely."*

"She'll kick both our asses, but you don't have to worry about us. We're going to be safe, all of us." He looked at Dylan as he spoke to them both. *"We've named our children. Would you like to know what their names are?"*

Jack groaned, and Dylan laughed. *"Our daughter is Abigail Corrine Bowen, and our son is Khan Jack Bowen. I wouldn't have either of them without the two of you coming together."*

"Sap," Jack said, but he could feel her pride, too. *"You have less than the count of fifteen. Jump when I say* one.*"*

When she got to five, they both stood up. At three they tensed to leap, and when she said one, they were gone. Khan had never been so terrified in his life when he landed and rolled. The river was not more than a few feet from them, and the rock wall she'd been talking about was less than that. Christ, she wasn't kidding about the timing.

After she disappeared around the next stand of trees, they took off after her, both of them running all out to beat her there. Just as they came up to the house, her headlights winked off and on through the trees. Dylan went to the back of the house, and he stayed in the front. Khan knew that there were at least two people in the house, and one of them was a wolf. Khan fucking hated wolves.

He reached for her as she got out of the truck and walked to the house. *"Two inside. One female and the other a male wolf. There are none in the front yard."*

"There are two back here." Dylan paused, and he could feel him getting pissed. *"Okay, just one back here, too."*

Khan might have laughed if he wasn't so afraid for her. She went up to the door and pulled her weapon. He could smell the silver from his station on the front porch. When she knocked, he moved up to the other side and waited.

Dylan knew where the key was to the back door. He was to shift, get the key, and unlock the door before shifting back to his cat and moving into the house from the rear. When the door opened, Khan stood at the ready.

"Hiya, girl. I thought I'd come by and see if you needed anything?" He knew it was her friend the moment she said "hiya." "Pretty night, huh? Wanna come out and hang with me a while?"

"I can't tonight. Maybe if you can come back later, we can talk then. I've sort of got some company." Jack nodded.

"Okay. Give me a hug, and I'll be on my way. I miss you in town." When Casey leaned forward, Jack wrapped her arms around her and jerked her forward. As soon as she was clear of the door, Khan moved in. He saw a flash of gray come at him, and then black. Khan knew that Dylan had gotten in.

It was over in seconds. The wolf was no match for Dylan's pissed off cat. As soon as he killed the wolf, Khan shot out the front after his brother and after the other wolf. Khan caught the darker wolf just as he was shifting and killed him instantly. Both men stood still in the moonlight and raised their noses to the sky. There were no other animals in the area.

They both padded to the truck, and Dylan jumped inside the bed and tossed down their bags. Lifting it in his mouth, he went to the slower smoother part of the river that ran by the house, and both of them leapt in. Neither wanted to go back home smelling like a dog.

"She had this right, you know." Khan looked at Dylan as he dressed. "Jack. She knew where the jump point was to the second. She's spent a great deal of time here."

Khan nodded, still remembering just how perfectly she'd timed it for them. "She would have been able to do this on her own, too. We helped, don't get me wrong, but she would have pulled it off."

Dylan nodded and pulled on his boots. "I'm in love with her. I know that you understand that, but I really am in love with her."

Khan nodded. "Yeah, don't kill me, but me, too. I love Caitlynne very much. But Jack…well, there is something so mean and loveable about her."

Both men were laughing as they walked back to the house. Jack was just coming out of the house with another woman when she saw them. She dropped everything and ran toward them. Dylan caught her in mid-jump as she wrapped herself around him.

"You hurt?" she asked. Dylan shook his head. "Good." She slapped him.

"What the fuck was that for?" Dylan sat her down as he rubbed his jaw. He didn't sound the least bit pissed and realized he'd expected the hit from her.

"You were supposed to wait for us if there were other wolves in the area. Not run off like some macho shit and take care of it all on your own. Do you have any idea how terrified I was that—?"

Dylan yanked her to him and kissed her. Khan looked over at the woman who'd come up beside him and smiled down at her. He could smell the wolf on her.

"Did the wolf hurt you?" She shook her head. "All the same I'd like for my brother to look you over when we get back to the house. He's a good doctor."

"And you think I'm not?" He looked at Jack when she laughed. "This ass just said I'm stupid."

"I most certainly did not. I said I wanted to have my brother look you over. I said he was a good doctor and you got all nasty like I insulted you or something."

"Down boy, she's just nervous. It's not every day that the big bad wolf comes knocking and then shifts into a man." Jack smiled at the two of them. "Casey Snow, I'd like for you to meet my leader, Khan Bowen. And this is my soon-to-be-husband, Dylan Bowen."

"Pleased to meet you." She shook both their hands. "What do we do about the mess in the living room? I'm not cleaning it up."

It took them nearly an hour to drag the body out and bury it. By the time he and Dylan had finished that, the girls had gotten the house cleaned up and locked down. Jack was setting the traps when he came up behind her.

"The wolf might have hurt your friend." She nodded. "How did he hurt her? If he raped her, I'll—"

"He didn't rape her, but she might need a few stitches in her leg. When he tried, she pulled a knife on him, and he rammed it in her leg when she dropped it getting away. It's not bad, but it is a little nasty."

He started to turn away when she stopped him. "Khan, I wanted to thank you again for coming with me. I might have gone in half-cocked, and having to make sure you two didn't put me on my best behavior. Thanks for that."

He nodded and headed to the other truck. He wasn't sure if she was telling him that she'd had to babysit them, and that's what kept her alive, or he'd just misheard her. He decided for the sake of feeling like an idiot and asking her to explain he'd just think he'd misheard her. Nodding to himself, he climbed in the truck with Dylan. Twenty minutes later, they were on the highway headed home.

~~~

The wolf was dead. He couldn't locate the human, and he still didn't have the woman and her information. He kicked the chair nearest him across the room and watched its broken pieces join the other splintered pieces on the floor. He was going to have to do something. The fucking trial was in two days. He had to find her and keep her from going to court, and he had to do it over the next two days.

Moving through the house, he didn't encounter anyone, human or vampire. He had a staff, small, but they should have been somewhere within the walls. When he stopped to listen, he realized that other than his own heartbeat there was no one within the walls, and only a few wolves inside the gates of his home. Closing his eyes, he reached for them and suddenly knew a touch of fear. They weren't there.

It took him several tries before he was able to summon one of the few who should have answered, and this man was not responding well. He sounded drugged and out of sorts.

Lucius materialized at his side to find the man dying and his body wasting away.

"What has happened to you?" When the man reached for him, Lucius backed away quickly. "Don't touch me."

"Poisoned, sir. We've all been poisoned." The human servant coughed, and great clods of blood poured from his mouth. "The butcher, sir. He sold us all tainted beef."

Tainted beef? He had no idea there was even a butcher in this small village, but to have one with tainted beef? He looked around for the first time in centuries at the place he'd called home. It was still as if he'd only just moved here.

There were no cars here, the streets so narrow that the horses and carts that had been so plentiful when he'd come here nearly two hundred years ago were the only thing that would pass in them. The buildings had thatched roofs and no glass in the openings of the windows. The man who now lay dead on the straw-filled mattress was wearing rough clothing; woolen, he supposed, and patched a great many times. Lucius stepped back and into the next room.

A fire burned low in the fireplace. A crock filled with water sat next to it with a ladle. The table was a worn sliver of wood over two cut logs, and the chairs were only another part of the same tree. Going into the street, he saw the same things. Flowers growing in large hewed logs, broken pottery, and rocks. Lucius sat on one of the many benches and thought about what he was seeing.

"They never moved on. I never let them, and they died because of that." Lucius called out for anyone around. There was no answer, as he had suspected. They were all dead. An entire village of people had died because he'd never told them to explore. Standing, he brushed off his clothing.

"They have deserted me is what they've done. In my greatest hour, they have left me to fend for myself." He moved toward the outskirts, occasionally calling for anyone to answer. "Stupid ignorant cattle. After all this time, they have left me alone and in my greatest hour. To hell with them all."

He turned back to the village and set fire to the first building, then several more. By the time he'd materialized in his home, the village was aflame, and as there was no one to put it out or to even call in the fire brigade, the town burned to ash by the next evening.

By the time he woke the following evening, he had come to a decision. He couldn't stay there any longer. He had no one to feed him, and the house would go to ruin if there were no villagers to make improvements. He knew just where he wanted to go, too.

To the capital. He would go to Washington DC and find the girl himself. And if on his journey he found the human, he would take care of him, as well. Satisfied with his new plans, Lucius went through the house looking for anything that would lead someone to realize that he was a vampire. When he found only a few items, he materialized at one of the finer hotels, in their best suite. He moved about the room and made adjustments, most of which had to with keeping his room dark when he rested. He also realized he'd have to find someone he could trust to watch over him.

But first things first...he had to find dinner. Walking along the streets, he found plenty to catch his eye, but very few that he felt were what he'd consider worthy of drinking from. It took him nearly an hour to find one human, and less than ten minutes to kill her. He took the first human he could find back to where the body of the first lay and killed her, as well. He had to find the human female, Crosby. When he found her, he decided that she would die, too. He'd had enough of this to last him for several lifetimes.

He looked the rest of the night for a suitable servant. What he found coming out of the large building just in front of him was even better.

The panther moved with the grace of a cat. Lucius loved the blood of all cats, but panther held a special kind of love. It was the first thing he'd fed on when he'd turned. It had filled his cells like nothing he'd had since. He moved behind the man and was ready to touch him when he turned suddenly.

He was young, probably in his early to mid-twenties. His face was a sculpture's dream…sloped nose and high cheek bones. His eyes were that of his kind, dark and beautifully surrounded by thick lashes. Lucius did enjoy the occasional male in his bed, but not as much as he did their counterpart. But he would make an exception for this one.

"You will come to me." The boy shook his head. "I did not ask. I said you will come to me."

Again he shook his head, and Lucius found himself proud that the panther, a mere child to him, thought to throw off his compulsion. Lucius reached out his hand for him and watched as he struggled. But in the end, he came to him.

"My brothers, my parents, they're expecting me." Lucius nodded as he folded him into his arms. "I don't think this is a good idea."

"Of course it's not. But it's much too late for you now." He took him to his room and let him look around. "You stay here with me tonight, and in the morning, I will set you free. Would you like that?"

The boy nodded. "I'd like to call my mom. She'll be worried, and I hate to worry them. There's a bunch of stuff going on at home, and I really would hate to have her worry."

"Later. You may call them later." Lucius sat in the chair and watched his lover. "You would like something to eat, perhaps?"

He declined, but Lucius ordered him a meal anyway. He knew growing boys were always hungry, and this one would be no exception. When the meal came, Lucius helped the boy sit after dismissing the waiter. The manager had come, too, to see what he was doing in the suite, but Lucius had straightened him out as well.

As the boy ate, Lucius moved up behind him and pulled him into a web. It was one he used all the time, where the human—or, in this case, panther—would think that Lucius really was their lover, and would enjoy anything and everything he did to them.

He nipped at the back of his throat and drank a small drink from him. He nearly climaxed then, because the boy was a pureblood. Licking along his neck to his shoulder, Lucius nipped him again and again, leaving a trail of blood running down his back to soak the shirt.

"Take off your clothes. I wish to see what I shall have tonight." He stood up, and Lucius undressed him. He lovingly folded his clothing and put it on the end of the bed. He wasn't sure why he did this, as the boy was going to be dead by sunrise, but it made the boy smile, and he was glad for that.

"I will take you now. Are you finished eating?" The boy nodded but hesitated. "What is it? Do you wish more to eat?"

"My mom. I want to call my mom." Frustration ran along Lucius's skin, and he looked at the boy. "You said later I could call her. Please, my mom will worry."

He moved toward the naked boy and threw him to the bed. Leaping on him so he couldn't shift, Lucius flipped him to his back and held him down.

"I've had enough waiting. I want you now." Freeing his cock, he leaned over the boy. He wanted to take him hard, but the blood was seeping from his earlier bites, and he let his fangs drop and bit deep into his neck.

Blood poured from the pounding pulse. As his struggles got weaker, Lucius had a moment of regret, but the blood was a more powerful lure than the body. Drinking until he felt sick from it, he moved off him and to the side of the bed, not bothering to seal the wounds. As soon as he bled out, Lucius showered and dressed again. He wrapped him in the spread beneath him and dropped him in the alley just behind the building he'd found him in. He looked up and laughed. The Central Intelligence office was about to get a very large surprise in the morning.

Chapter Twelve

"You can't see him." Dylan tried to shove past the man at the front of the crime scene. "We have to look for clues, sir, and if you go in there, we'll never catch the killer."

Dylan nodded. He had heard from the hotel where he and Jack had checked into last night that a young man had been killed later that night. Marshall had told him it was a panther. Dylan had left his room to come and see if there was anything he could do to help. His brother came up beside him.

"I knew him. He was going to come out to the house to run with me soon." Dylan knew that Reed was hurting. To lose another of their kind was a horrible blow, but to lose a friend was harder.

"I'm trying to get back to see if I can learn anything, but I'm being stonewalled." Reed whistled through his teeth. "Was that really necessary?"

Reed grinned as the same police officer came to him. Before he could open his mouth, Reed showed him his badge. He nodded to him.

"This man was sent down here to help Mrs. Bowen with the investigation. She said that anyone dropped on her fucking front step would get the best. He is the best. Do you think you can get him back to look around?"

The man looked more terrified than impressed. When he told Dylan to follow him, Reed came as well. Dylan was impressed and, obviously, so was the cop. He spoke in low tones, but Dylan had no problem hearing him.

"You work for Mrs. Bowen, huh?" Reed said yes. "I hear she's a real ball buster. Good at her job and all, but a real ball buster."

"She can be, but she's fair, too. I love working for her." Dylan knelt down by the boy and reached out to touch him. A pair of gloves slapped him on the shoulder.

"Gotta wear these. We have to protect everyone from blood borns, you know." The man shook them at Dylan again. "Seriously. You have to put them on. Naked man in the alley might have AIDs or something like hepatitis."

Dylan took the gloves and "accidently" dropped one on the boy's neck. Making sure he ran his finger along the bites there, he pulled on the glove and thanked the other cop. He had all he needed, but made a show of looking him over. When he stood up, the first cop came toward him with Reed in tow.

"I would like you to make sure that a report is sent to Mrs. Bowen when you talk to the coroner. I will contact her and let her know to call my office." Reed stepped away, coughing. Dylan knew he was laughing, but what the fuck else was he supposed to say? Thanks, but I know everything because I touched the saliva that the fucking vamp left behind? Yeah, that would go over well.

They both entered the CIA building, and, again, Reed cleared the way for him to get in. As they were riding up in the elevator, Dylan told him that he was proud of him. He laughed.

"What that cop said about Caitlynne is true. She is a fucking ball buster. Some days all I want to do is call someone to come here and get me. She's a pain in the ass."

"But," Dylan asked him, "you love her and the job you do for her, right? You did a great job back there and for Caitlynne. For all her ball busting, she speaks highly of you to others, and to Mom and Dad. She told them they'd done a very good job of raising you."

Reed flushed but said nothing. As the elevators opened, there stood Caitlynne and Khan, but the only person he had eyes for was Jack. She came to him when he opened his arms for her. He was very glad he'd let her talk him into coming to the city last night.

"He was killed by a vampire. He wanted him because he was a panther, and his excitement grew when he realized he was full blooded. His family will have to be notified."

"I've already got someone going to the house now. I didn't want them to have to come here and identify him. That's why I sent Reed." Reed nodded at her. "Christ, that poor kid and his family."

"There's something else. He's looking for Mann." That had them all looking at him as he sat on the couch and Jack beside him. "I don't know why, but he's looking for him. He seems to think that the man owes him and can't believe that he's left him with a job half finished. He is also looking for Jack."

"I don't know any vampires," Jack practically shouted. Then in a much lower voice, she continued, "Hell, I didn't know you guys existed until last month. What does he want me for?"

Dylan pulled her into his lap and held her. He had to tell her, but he was so afraid for her. Not that she couldn't handle herself, but because the man wanted her dead, not just to feed from her.

"He wants to get Small in the White House, and is afraid that with the information that Jack has on him, not only will he not be able to help him, but he'll be shot for treason." Caitlynne stood up and went to her desk.

"Did you happen to catch why he wants Small in the White House?" Dylan nodded. "Please tell me that he doesn't think the bastard is going to be president after what he's done? He can't be that stupid."

"No. It's something to do with the White House being cursed, or he is. It's a little fuzzy when you read so little of someone. But this vampire, Lucius…no last name…thinks that once Small gets inside he'll be able to send all the plans and any other strategic information back to him, and he'll be rich. His words, not mine."

"And do what with it?" Khan looked as confused as he felt. "Does he think that Small has some hidden way to get in and out of here without anyone noticing he's carting out large files? Or does he think that he can fax it all to him?"

There was a brisk knock on the door before it opened. Everyone stood, and Caitlynne and Jack drew their weapons. The man smiled at them and looked at Khan. He bowed low and stood.

"You're their leader?" the man said. Khan nodded. "I would ask your permission to speak to you all, if you please. You will benefit greatly if I were able to."

"You. I know you." Jack stepped forward. "You were there that night. The night I was shot."

"Yes. Very good, miss. But I cannot tell you anything until I am given permission. He must allow me to speak as you all belong to him." Dylan reached out and pulled Jack to him before she said something stupid like she belonged to no one. "Sir? I ask your permission to speak."

"You have it. I don't know who you are, but if you had anything to do with Jack getting hurt that night, I'm going to tear you apart." Dylan stepped forward as well, and Jack stepped in front of them both.

"He saved me." She offered him a chair. "I didn't know where I was. I was hurting and dizzy, and he showed me the way. He even said...you said you'd take care of my car for me. Make it so that no one would see it."

"Correct. How lovely that you remember me. I say, I never thought you'd make it, but here you are." He sat down and looked around. "You will need to rest a bit please. I have a story to tell. One that will help you all to understand."

Everyone sat, and he nodded. The man was dressed like he'd just come from a renaissance fair. His hair was snowy white, and he had a beard that seemed to dance along his chin. And Dylan couldn't read him. When he looked at him, Dylan heard him.

"You should know that I have picked you for her. And only you." Dylan looked at Jack. *"Yes, her. She is the only one for you, and the only one that can stop this madness. She will need help, but she will be the one to stop it. Are you willing to help her?"*

"I would die for her. She's my life. I cannot, nor will I let anyone hurt her again." The man smiled.

"Then you will have her," he said to him before turning to the others. "I have come to tell you a story. The vampire and I met many, many years ago. Long before this building was here, long before any of you were here, either. We met in a bar, and he was telling me how he would rule the kingdom. I had no idea at the time which kingdom he spoke of, but we had embarked on a tale, him and me."

"Wait. I'm sorry, but how did you get in here? And who are you?" Caitlynne looked around, still holding her gun. "I asked not to be disturbed, yet here you are."

"Yes, here I am. But you will need what I have to say. And I am Wizard Jacob." He stood and shook her hand and everyone else's. "I must say, I have waited for this time for so long. I'm glad to be having it finished."

"You said wizard." Jacob nodded at him. "As in magical? You're a wizard, and you met with Lucius. Were you with him when he killed the young panther?"

"No. I was not, sadly. I was with Lucius when he was a mere child of a vampire. It was in the year of our Lord eighteen fifty-three. This world had just started to live, you see, and I came on an adventure. I got a bit more than I'd bargained for, I'm afraid." He sat back in his chair. "He wished to run these grand states and do it from the White House. So, I fixed it so that neither he nor any of his kind could enter. Ever."

"Why?" Jack looked around the room, embarrassment on her face. "The White House was barely there back then. What did he hope to gain?"

"Money? Fame? Who knows with a man such as him. But I did fix him. And now he feels that he has a way to override my magic."

Dylan looked around the room. No one was speaking, but he would bet a lot was being said. He glanced at his brother, then at Jack. She looked the most confused of all. But Jacob looked…well, he was going to say happy, but delighted came to mind, too.

"You say he wants to override your magic." Jacob nodded at Jack's question. "Then that's between the two of you, it seems. I mean, I'll help you because I'd be dead if you hadn't been there for me, but I seriously don't have a clue what this has to do with us."

He laughed. "You are very clever, you are. It has to do with you because you have the key to his downfall. Not any magic, though it is possible you have a bit. But it's what you have in your heart. It's pure, did you know that? Few humans…well, few of any species…have a pure heart, but you possess one. As does your mate."

"I don't think I'm going to offer up my heart to this ass, but thanks anyway." He laughed at her again, and Jack bristled. "You could help me understand a lot more if you did a great deal less laughing and more telling. And I'm not stupid."

"Nay, you are not. You are very…what is the word? Ah yes, street smart. That is his downfall. When you face him, and you shall, you'll need all of that." Jacob looked around the room. "All the people in this room, this building even, could face the vampire and maybe outwit him, but you will be the one who will destroy him. And he must be destroyed, no matter the outcome of the man he wishes to manipulate."

"What did you do?" Dylan hadn't realized he'd spoke out loud until everyone turned to him. "You said you made it so he couldn't go into the White House. What did you do?"

"I spread a bit of myself around the bricks and mortar so that it would hold. Then when they've done renovations, I came again. It is a grand place, is it not? All those lovely rooms and the president; this man is a great deal like you." He looked at Marshall and nodded. "Yes, I do suppose you do know that. But I have misplaced myself. A bit of my magic and my blood around the rooms to safeguard them and the people it is there to protect. But I can't keep humans out. If this man Small returns to the building and does as Lucius wishes, all will be lost."

"So why not just make sure that Small doesn't enter?" Khan asked. Jacob shook his head. "Because…because he'll simply find another sap."

"Correct. Now you see what must be done." He stood up. "I will leave you now. You have much to—"

"Hold on there, buddy," Jack said. "I don't see anything. You come in here spouting magic and blood. You tell me I have a pure heart, then leave? No. That's not the way it goes." Jack stared at him. "You want something from me. I want something in return."

"And what would that be?" His voice had hardened. Jacob folded his arms over his chest and glared at her.

"You keep them safe. The Bowens, you keep them all safe no matter what happens with Lucius. You have to promise me that or I don't do it. I can't do it." Dylan started to speak, but Jacob raised his hand to him, and he was unable to move.

"All Bowens? You wish all of them safe?" Jacob asked. She nodded. "Then we have a deal. I shall keep them safe. You'll help me, then?"

"Yes." She put out her hand, and he took it to pull her to him. Dylan was set free, and he moved to the man. Jacob let her go before he told him to. Then he pulled him to his body for a hug, as well.

"You'll marry her today," drifted through his mind. *"Marry her, and she becomes one of you. I cannot protect her without it."*

~~~

Jack was nearly at a run to keep up with Dylan. She had no idea where they were going, but he was in an all fired hurry to get there. She finally jerked on his hand and made him stop. This was stupid.

"You make me run to your brother's house to borrow a dress you made me put on and shoes that are pinching the crap out of my toes. Then you leave the place like it's on fire, and now we're running like we're being chased across town. What the fuck is wrong with you?" She leaned against him to pull off her shoe and massage her foot. "I'm not going any farther unless you explain yourself."

"We're getting married." She looked at him. "Now. Right now, we're getting married. I want you in my life, and I don't want to wait any longer."

She looked at him and could see he was serious. "You think you might have told me? Or someone else at your brother's house? We were at that office for over an hour, and you couldn't have told me then?"

"They're at the courthouse now, my family is. I told them before I asked you to get dressed up and they left already." He reached for her hand again, and she backed away. "If you want a real wedding later, we'll have one as big as you like. But my family is waiting on us."

"Does this have anything to do with making me a Bowen?" He flushed. "It doesn't work that way, Dylan. Making me carry your last name doesn't make me a Bowen. It makes me your wife. Especially if you do it this way."

"I don't understand the difference." She didn't think he would. "Tell me, Jack, because I want you as my wife for a long time. If this is how it works, then we're going to do it."

"Do you love me? I mean, really love me?" He said he did. "But you don't trust me. Because that's the only reason I can see that you'd whisk me across town without telling me why. Did you think I'd get there and say 'well, he's gone to this much work, I'll do it'? You have to know me better than that."

He leaned against the tree near them. "He told me to marry you. Jacob did. He said to marry you today or he couldn't protect you."

"I see." She turned to go back to the house. She didn't want to start their life together like this. When she took several steps, he said her name. She turned back to him.

"I had it set up for tomorrow. Our getting married. I had my parents come up today so that we'd be all set for tomorrow morning. I have tickets for us." He reached into his jacket pocket. "See? I bought us tickets to honeymoon in Paris. I wanted everything to be perfect. Monica helped me order flowers; Khan even had my suit dry cleaned. All for tomorrow."

"We can wait," she said as she walked back to him. "I can wait until tomorrow if you want to."

"No. I've...I need you, Jack. More than I thought possible, I need you. Having you as my wife one day earlier means I get one more day with you as my bride than if we waited until tomorrow."

"You're a sap." He nodded. "But I love you." The applause startled them both. She looked at the crowd around them and flushed. They should have been a little more discreet in their argument. Then Dylan picked her up and swung her around to the pleasure of the people around them. Then he put her down and dropped to his knee.

"Jack Crosby, will you please marry me today? I have it all set up so that all you have to do is say 'yes' now and 'I do' later." He nodded.

"Go on, girl. The man is getting his pants dirty for you. And he's too purty of a thing to be all mussed." The older woman cackled. "Though if I was younger, I'd muss him but good."

Laughing, Jack said, "Yes." When Dylan stood up, he kissed her, then went to the older woman and kissed her, as well. They were off again, and this time she was dragging him.

They were all there, all the Bowens, including Monica and the babies. Marshall was there to make sure there were no glitches. Warren sent her three dozen daisies, because she didn't strike him as a rose sort of woman. And just before the ceremony started, Jacob showed up.

"There you have it. You'll be a Bowen, and all will be right with the world." She looked at him and smiled. "You know, don't you, lass?"

"That you would have saved me anyway?" He winked. "Yes, you old fart. You had to put the fear of losing me into him. But you were wrong. He'd already had it planned for tomorrow."

Jacob nodded and kissed her on the cheek. After shaking hands with everyone, he left them with a gift. He told them not to open it until they were back to their own home together in Ohio.

Chapter Thirteen

Kirby looked over the letter again. He thought it was all there, but he knew that he'd missed a few things. Finding small mistakes, easily fixed, he was finally finished. Hitting the send button was all he had left to do, so he sat back and looked around the room.

"Christ." He had no idea how long he'd been sitting there. He thought it might have been only a day, but when he rubbed his hand over his chin he knew it had to have been more. Getting up, he nearly tripped over his own pants. They were hanging on him like he'd lost a great deal of weight. Going to the mirror, he almost didn't recognize himself.

His eyes were bloodshot and dry. His hair, usually so well kept, looked as if some small rodent had taken up residency in it. It was ratted and all over his head. His face was haggard, cheeks sunken, and whiskers long and curled so that he looked homeless and starved. Pulling off his clothes, meaning to get into the shower, the stench made him gag and his eyes water. He'd lost weight, too. More than he could afford. He looked like he'd not eaten in—

Kirby went to the television that hadn't been on since the interview he'd seen with Bowen the Bitch. Thumbing through the stations until he found the weather station, he sat down hard on the bed. He had to watch the time and date flash three times over before he could take it in. He'd been there for six days. Six whole days writing and sleeping. Standing up, he went back to the bathroom, turned on the spray to the hottest setting, and went to his luggage. Kirby pulled out his first aid kit and got scissors.

Trying not to look at himself but at the task at hand, Kirby cut away the beard first. He didn't know enough about his hair to cut it himself, so he debated for several seconds before deciding he'd wait until he got out of the shower. If it still looked horrible, he'd hack at it until he couldn't any longer. Getting into the stall, he scrubbed his body three times, feeling better with every wash. By the time he got out, he realized he was hungry.

Shaving proved to be exhausting. There was so much hair still on his face that he'd cut himself twice pretty good and had to change out razors halfway through. When he finished he looked marginally better, but not the Kirby Mann that he'd made himself into.

He was dressing when the door to the room exploded open. He knew this day was coming and was glad now that he'd— Damn it. He'd not hit send.

"Hello, human. I have been looking for you." Lucius walked into the room and looked around. "You've become a pig. This room looks as if you've been here for months and not even had anyone clean up after you. You've let yourself go to ruin."

Kirby laughed. Not smart, he supposed, but he couldn't help it. Lucius couldn't have been closer to the truth. The vampire looked at him with disgust. Kirby picked up his shoes and took them to the chair he'd been sitting in for days.

"I had some things to straighten out. And I needed peace and quiet." Kirby leaned over and pulled on his shoe. "And the house smelled of death."

"You will know that smell soon enough, too. You have disappointed me greatly, and we had a deal. What do you think I do to people who do not—?"

"You killed my wife and daughter, didn't you?" Lucius looked shocked, then smiled. "I thought so. You disappoint me, as well. We had a bargain of sorts, too, and you fucked it up when you killed my Sally and Karrie. They were the only things that kept me in line. When I figured out you'd murdered them, I decided to quit you."

Kirby leaned down to pull on his other shoe, put his hand on the computer, and moved the mouse. When he reached down to tie his shoe, he could see that he had no connection. He nearly cried out. Mother fuck, could nothing go right?

"You knew they were dead? How? She couldn't call to you. The child…she was nothing but a drain on you. You have thought yourself the same thing." Kirby moved the mouse again, sweat beading on his forehead. "I gave you something you have wished for."

"I never wished for their death." He got a connection and moved the mouse again. But the computer was thrown away from him before he could try to send again.

"You wished them gone." Lucius had shoved the computer to the floor, and Kirby glanced at it to see that it was still running. When Lucius slashed at him, Kirby knew he'd fucked up royally. He should have sent it when he finished. Now no one would know.

He dropped to his knees, his blood pouring from his throat. Lucius sat in his chair and watched him as if he was a fireworks display, and he was waiting for the grand finale. Kirby thought maybe he was.

"You should have done what I told you. You'd still be dead, but I would have made it quicker." He laughed as Kirby fell fully to the floor. "Maybe not. I do love a grand death scene."

The keys were there. Letting go of his ruined throat, Kirby tried to see the keys. His vision was blurred, and he was fading quickly. Blindly, he touched where he thought he needed to be and closed his eyes. He knew he was as good as dead, but worked at opening them once more, just to see if he'd been successful. The words, *"Your message has been sent. View message"* were the best words of his life. He heard Lucius cursing.

"What is that thing? What does it mean you've sent something? What have you done? Bring it to me." Kirby smiled. He could barely move, much less bring back an email that should have been taken care of years—no, decades—ago. Lucius continued to scream at him to stop the machine.

Kirby closed his eyes as he felt his belly spill out onto the dirty floor. There was no pain now, only a sense of accomplishment, something he'd not felt, he realized, for many years.

~~~

Dylan shook hands with his family and tried to move his new wife, his only wife, toward the door. He had made them reservations at the Grand after Jacob had left, and now all he had to do was get her there. He wanted her there ten minutes ago. She looked at him again when he pulled her to the door. Khan laughed.

"He wants to consummate the marriage. Don't blame him. I felt the same way after I married Monica." The woman in question hit her husband. "Okay, she wanted to. Nearly raped me when we got into the elevator, too, if I remember right."

Monica handed him one of the twins and told him to shut up. She moved toward the newlyweds, pushing them to the door. She had a way about her that made Dylan glad she was his leader, too.

"Go now, before someone else comes in here and asks you about where you've been." Jack had been questioned by everyone. "I'll take care of the reception for tomorrow night. It's still on, right?"

"Yes." Dylan kissed her cheek. "Thank you for this. I know that I sort of messed up your plans to—"

"You married her, and that's what we all wanted. I love you both dearly, and am glad you're together." Someone called for Jack, and Monica told them to wait. "If you don't go now, I may shift and eat the lot of them."

Laughing, they ran out the door and into the waiting limo. As soon as the door closed, Dylan pulled her over his lap and kissed her. She responded just like he'd hoped she would. Christ, the woman had him panting before the car moved.

He took her nipple through the bodice of the dress. He felt it harden, and he nipped at it until she moaned. Reaching behind her, he pulled the zipper tab down and peeled the dress off her, leaving her arms caught in it.

"You distract me. I want to nibble, and when you touch me, I can't think." She moaned again when he unhooked her bra and filled his hands with her. "So warm and all mine. When we get to the hotel, I'm going to make love to you. Softly, slowly, until you can't move."

"Dylan, I'm not going to make it to the hotel. Please, take me now." He laughed and suckled at her breast harder. "Dylan."

Her voice was breathless, and he loved her that way, but he could tell she was close, and he thought if he took the edge off for her she'd let him do what he wanted once they got there. Running his hand up her thigh, he slipped his finger under her panties.

"If I let you come, will you behave?" She shook her head. "Then you'll have to suffer. I'll have the driver pull over, and I'll sit up front with him until we get there."

"I fucking hate you right now." She moved over him, riding him through their clothes until she looked down at him. "All right, but it had better be worth my time."

He rolled her to the seat and lifted her dress up. Her panties were soaked, and he could smell her. Sliding his fingers up and down her thigh, he looked at her.

"You can't scream. The driver will hear you. Can you be quiet?" She shook her head, then reached for the tiny purse that one of the maids had shoved at her before they left the house. She put it in her mouth and nodded. He smiled at her.

Leaning down slowly, he licked a path along her thigh. Her skin was hot, and he wished now that he had more time. Reaching to the driver, he told him to drive around the city until he asked him to take them to the hotel.

"You're going to come quickly, aren't you?" She nodded and moaned when he kissed her bare flesh above her panties. "I can't wait to get you back to the hotel where you can scream all you want. Do you have any idea what that does to me to hear you shout out my name as you come? Fucking fantastic."

He reached up under her panties at the hips and pulled them down slowly. She rocked up to meet his mouth when he leaned toward his goal. Pulling them completely off her, he slipped them into his pocket and cupped her ass, lifting her up slightly.

Running his tongue over her from gate to clit, she shivered in his hands. Dylan wanted more, but he wanted her to suffer a little. She was going to get relief when he wasn't. Pulling her clit into his mouth, he worried the small nubbin until her fingers curled in his hair.

"Please, Dylan. You're killing me. I want you to be inside of me. I love the feeling of you there. Hot and thick." He sat up. She reached for his pants and jerked at his belt.

"Let me before you injury me." Laughing, he opened his belt and undid his pants. Pulling them down over his hips, he picked her up and put her over him. She was so wet she soaked him immediately.

Fisting his cock, he told her to rise up. Guiding her slowly down over him, he nearly came when she rolled her hips. He gripped her hips hard to have her stop, but she smiled at him and dropped hard over his cock.

"Christ." He held her still, not wanting to come so soon. "You said you'd behave. This is not what I had in mind when I told you I'd give you relief."

"We both need this." She moved despite him holding her. "I want to ride you slow. I want to come with your teeth at my throat."

Her hips moved again, slower and smoother. He held her and helped her get a good rhythm for them. Taking her nipple in his mouth, he feasted on her. She held him to her breast, and Dylan nipped none too gently at her.

"Dylan, I'm coming. Yes, I'm coming." She dropped her head to his shoulder and screamed against him. Her shoulder was so close that he didn't even hesitate but licked along the point where her neck met and bit her hard.

Dylan rolled her to her back, and she wrapped her legs around him. He never let go with his canines, but sank his teeth deeper. She screamed again as he pounded harder, taking her over and over until his cock exploded inside of her. Dylan wanted her with him forever. He wanted her to be by his side in all ways. He kissed her gently and looked down at her.

"I can convert you if you want. Make you into a panther. But there are risks. Plenty of them. You could die if not done right, and you could be very ill after it. Do you want to be like me?" She nodded. "It's dangerous, but Christ, the thought of running with you through the woods with me is what I want for us."

"What do you need from me? Anything? Please convert me." He licked the wound at her throat and sat her up so that she was sitting over him again.

"I'll need to bite you hard. Harder than I've ever done before. You'll hurt so badly that you'll beg me to stop. If I do, you may die." He pulled her to him so that her head rested on his forehead. "I can't lose you, Jack. You're everything to me. I love you so very much."

"I want this as badly as you. Monica and Caitlynne both said it's dangerous and scary, but please do this for me. For us." He nodded. "When do you want to do this? I want it done tonight. What better way to start our lives together than like that."

He kissed her and asked her if she was sure. Her kiss told him that she was more than sure, and he told her that they needed to get dressed. He wanted to make her his in more ways than just his wife.

They entered the hotel twenty minutes later and went up to their room. It was the bridal suite, and after the man who had brought up their bags left, Dylan started to have second thoughts about the whole thing. Wandering around the room, he started talking about the conversation with Jacob.

"What do you think of the wizard? You think what he says about all that stuff with Lucius is true. I mean, if you think about it, he's pretty old. I know of a couple of vampires that have been around for a while, but I've never heard of a wizard."

"He said he's older than Lucius. Much he told me, but not how old. I don't know why, but I do believe him." She sat on the bed and bounced. "Come here and sit with me and tell me what's wrong."

"Nothing's wrong." But he didn't go near the bed. "I was just having a conversation with you."

He heard the bite of his voice and took a deep breath. He wasn't even sure why he didn't want to talk to her about it. He went to the window and looked down over the city. They could see the Pentagon from there, and he watched as the lights twinkled.

"All right. Then we'll play this your way." She stood up and grabbed her overnight case. "When you're finished sulking and feeling sorry for yourself, I'll be in the tub. I have a desire to wash you off me."

The door slammed shut, and he winced. He hadn't meant to make her mad, and now that he had, he wanted to make it up to her. She was his wife, damn it, and this was their first night together as man and wife, and he had fucked it up. He looked out the window again and thought about what he'd done.

"Fuck." He grabbed up the phone and called room service. "I would like to have dinner sent to our room, please, and champagne. Also, do you think it's possible to get a couple dozen lilies brought up?"

"Yes, sir. Right away on the flowers. What is it you and the missus would like to eat? The kitchen is always open, and we have a large variety of dinners to choose from." He reached for the menu.

After he ordered, he asked for it to be brought up as soon as possible. The man said it would be less than half an hour on the flowers and food. Dylan told him that would be great and hung up. He called Monica next.

"I need to know what happened when Khan converted you. I want…we're thinking about it, and I don't have any answers other than the bits and pieces I've gotten from you and Caitlynne." Dylan sat down and closed his eyes. "I pissed her off, and I need to make it up to her."

"On your wedding night? Oh, Dylan, you idiot." He didn't need her help if she was going to be nasty, and told her so. "You want my help, you'll bring it down a notch. And if this is how you pissed off Jack, I don't blame her."

He took a deep breath. "I'm sorry. I asked her if she wanted to be converted, and she said yes, and now I'm…. Christ, I don't want to lose her. What if I fuck this up for us, and I lose her?"

Monica told him step by step how Khan had converted her. By the time she was finished, he was more terrified than before. She told him that if he loved her, and she was sure that he did, he'd not screw it up.

"But you have to remember that you can't stop no matter how much she begs you to. If you do, she'll bleed to death." She was quiet for several seconds. "You're going to do it tonight, aren't you?"

"Yes. She wants to start our life out right. What the hell was I thinking even suggesting this?" Monica laughed. "You know this really isn't all that funny. I want this to work."

"Then it will. And the reason I'm laughing is because you being unsure is funny to me. You're the cockiest, most self-assured Bowen of all of you. I mean it. You do what you want, when you want, to who you want. It's just great to see you so lost. And you've no idea how proud you've made me by asking for my help."

A few minutes later he hung up. The knock at the door startled him for a few seconds before he remembered the food. Having the waiter set it up on the nice table, Dylan tipped him and took the flowers to the bathroom door and knocked.

"Go away." He cringed. He'd fucked up really badly. He knocked again and turned the handle. It was locked. Leaning his head against the door, he tried to talk to her.

"I'm sorrier than you can ever know. I screwed up, but I'm willing to start over." The door jerked open so quickly he nearly fell into the room. But his tongue got all tangled up around what he was going to say as she stood there, as beautiful and as naked as he'd ever seen her.

"You pissed me off." He could see that he had and nodded. "It's our fucking honeymoon and you pissed me off, so now I've been sitting in this tub for the past thirty minutes crying. I hate to fucking cry."

"I love you." He shoved the flowers at her and took a step toward her. "When we got here, all I could think about was what would happen if I messed up. If I did something wrong and I hurt you, or killed you even. I couldn't do that to you. I couldn't do that to us."

"Then why the fuck did you even bring it up?" He nearly shrugged but thought better of it. She didn't look to be armed, but he wasn't sure she still couldn't hurt him. Dylan reached over, grabbed a towel, and handed it to her. He couldn't think with her like that.

"Can you please put this on?" He tried his most charming grin. "I can't think when you look like a sex goddess to me."

She snatched the towel and, thankfully, wrapped it around herself and not his throat. "Is all you think about sex? I swear to Christ, I'm going to be pregnant if you don't learn to keep that thing under some control."

The thought of her swollen with his child had him reach for the doorjamb. Pregnant. He'd never thought of her carrying his child, their child, and realized that he wanted that very much. He reached for her, and she slapped his hand away. Well, that might happen if he ever got to touch her again. Dylan thought about what Monica had told him about changing Jack.

"When I do this to you, you're going to be in a great deal of pain for a while. Monica said that it hurts more than giving birth to twins. She said to tell you that if you think about what it's going to be like after, after the conversion is over, then that helps. Not a great deal, but it does help." He watched her still as he continued. "I have to bite you, as I've said, but I have to do it deeply, tear into your body as if I'm trying to kill you. That terrifies me more than I can say to you."

"You're afraid of killing me." He nodded. "I'm very strong and healthy. I know that helps. I talked to Caitlynne about it. Well, she cornered me and told me about it. She, too, said that it hurts, but she thought it was the most wonderful thing in the world. I personally think she's a sadist, but I'm not positive."

He laughed and reached for her again, and she came to him this time. "Do you still want to try, baby? I'm no less afraid for you, but I do want to try this."

Looking up at him, she smiled. "I want to try. And so you know, if you kill me, I'm coming back as a wolf and beating the shit out of you."

"Deal." He held her for several more minutes, then they moved to the bedroom. He loved this woman very much. After helping her into her robe, they sat down to eat, and he told her everything that Monica had told him. By midnight, they were ready to begin.

Chapter Fourteen

Lucius found her. Now all he had to do was get her to him and to have her bring him what he needed to get Small free. He rubbed his hands together and thought of how nicely and neatly things were coming together. Frowning, he thought of the human again.

He'd tried to make the contraption work after the human had bled out. There was no hope for it. The machine would not do as he'd commanded it. He'd finally thrown it against the wall and destroyed it in much the same fashion he had the human. And he had destroyed him.

It had taken him several minutes to come back to himself. After his beast, a horrible creature even to him, had come forth, Lucius had lost control of himself. He'd not done that in many years and had actually been a little afraid. But the destruction was more than he'd ever seen from himself before.

The human was shredded. Parts of his body were strewn about the hotel room and had splattered on the windows and walls so badly that he'd been sure that he'd killed more than one person. But it had only been the one human. And before he could clean it up, he'd had to leave and feed, with the idea to come back and put things back to pristine order. With, of course, the exception of the human.

But he'd been too long. Someone from the management staff of the establishment had been there when he'd returned with all manner of police. He watched for a long while, wondering if they would know it was him, hoping really that they would say his name, but they only said unknown assailant. Lucius even thought of showing himself but didn't at the last minute, knowing that he had to get to Small and the woman.

And now he had her. Or at least knew where she was. Getting to her was proving to be tricky, even for him. The girl had more silver on her person than he'd ever seen a human have before. But she would prove to be no challenge once he was able to get her.

The man she was with was a panther. Lucius had actually thought of taking him and making her do as he wanted by holding the man in his grasp. He had a feeling, though, that the girl wouldn't play fair. She seemed to be a little unstable, and worst yet, as a female he knew she'd be unpredictable. He didn't need a complication right now. Time was running short.

He materialized near the place where he knew her to be and waited. She'd have to come out of the house sooner or later, as would the man she was with. He shivered when he thought of the spell he'd nearly crossed when he'd tried to go onto the ground where she was. The place had been warded against him, specifically him. That bastard wizard had been up to his old tricks again.

Lucius had tried to kill him off several times over the years. The man had been crafty and free with his magic. Every time Lucius thought he was getting closer to his goal of ruling over the human, the wizard would appear, and he'd be thwarted once again. He was going to kill him as soon as he freed Small and had all he needed. And what Lucius wanted was power and money. With that he knew he'd be king.

Bored with watching the house, Lucius moved back to his hotel room. He only had a few hours before sunrise, and he thought he'd find a human to fuck and to feed from before going to sleep. But when he got there, his room had been touched. Someone had been inside of it and had…cleaned it.

Looking around the room, he'd been amazed at the touches that he'd discovered. He thought about his house in the village where he'd grown up and the townspeople there, and he realized that he'd never been this clean before, his things so straight, and most of all, his sleeping chamber so nice smelling. He realized then that his bed had been neatly made twice now. Every time he left for the night, he'd come back to it made. Sitting down on the edge of the bed, he thought about the spotty workmanship that his servants had done all the while he'd been keeping them around him.

Lucius remembered at the last second that he couldn't go back to the village and make them pay for their laziness. They were all dead. Happy about that, and relieved actually that he'd not have to sully himself with them, he realized that it was now too late for him to leave. Closing up the room, he laid down. He smiled, thinking of the girl and all he was going to do to her once he had her.

There was no doubt that he was going to kill her. But he was going to make her suffer. Not like he'd done to the human, but suffer greatly. He was going to take her first. Then when she was still sated from sex, he was going to cut into her slowly and watch her die. A kind of killing that he'd perfected over the years, one that took time, energy as well as a high tolerance to hear someone scream and scream a great deal. He was going to enjoy killing the girl.

Closing his eyes, he felt the sun take him. The higher in the sky it raised, the more his body began to shut down. Two hours after the first rays of the sun touched the earth, Lucius was dead to the world, quite literally.

~~~

Jack opened her eyes and quickly shut them again. The room was much too bright and too crowded. Opening them slowly, she looked at the people sitting around in different positions of sleep and frowned. She supposed that they had come to see if she was going to hurt Dylan again.

"How do you feel, my dear?" She looked over at George, her new father-in-law. "I heard that you had a very easy time of it. Dylan, however…well, he's been put to bed by his brother. He didn't take you hurting all that well, I'm afraid."

"He's a wuss. He kept telling me he was sorry, and I'd finally had enough." She looked around again at the sleeping people. "Is he still bleeding? I hadn't meant to slug him all that hard, but it was hard to concentrate on not screaming when he was speaking nonsense."

"So he said. No, he's not bleeding, but I wish I could have seen his face when you hit him." George roared with laughter. "I think you're going to have splendid children. I'm hoping that you're going to have a passel of them for me and the missus to spoil. But Dylan said that you made not a sound when he bit you. He said that it was what made him know it wasn't going to work, having an easy time at it and all. And I will think on the 'wuss' part. He is very touchy when someone calls him that." Jack tried to sit up but lay back again. "You'll be weak for a little while. I nearly said a few days, but I don't think you'll ever follow any rules that others put to you, will you?"

"Not if I can help it." She had heard George say that Dylan said he knew it wouldn't work. She wasn't a panther, and closed her eyes against the pain that caused her. She'd wanted it so badly. She turned to look at George when he cleared his throat.

"Are you hungry? I was about to go down and have a nice snack. If you were to go with me, I could have a bigger one and blame it on you. Corrine wants me to watch my weight. Says a fat panther is sloppy." He snorted, and she laughed softly. "I'll bring you something up if you'd prefer."

She sat up slowly. She didn't hurt now after all the pain she'd had before. She felt really good and amazingly hungry. When she stood up, George reached out for her but didn't touch her. She was getting used to that, the sort of no touching, yet helpful, way the men acted around her. Kissing, she'd figured out, was fine so long as you cleared it with the male. Hugging, too. But no lingering touches at all. They were halfway down the stairs when Monica joined them. She looked as fresh as a daisy.

"The babies woke me when they got hungry, otherwise I'd still be napping." She moved to the sink to wash up. Jack sat down, hunger beating at her. She leaned back in the kitchen chair and waited to get some energy before she tackled a snack. But Monica had it under control.

"I wanted a snack, and George said he'd help me down here. I asked him to join me, so I'll fix it." Monica shook her head. "I don't want to put anyone out. Just give me a—"

"Just please. I love to play in this big kitchen. And I remembered how I felt afterwards. I was tired for a week, I think. You just sit. Your energy will come back, and you'll feel really great. Especially after you shift."

"It didn't work." They both looked at her, and she looked at George. "You said that Dylan knew it wouldn't work. It didn't, right? That I didn't become like him? I'm simply a pain in the ass human."

"Oh no, dear. I'm terribly sorry. You're a panther. Well, you're more than likely going to be a pain in the ass human, as well, and I believe that trait will flow over into your cat, but that's for you and Dylan to work with. As a matter of fact, it worked very well, and quickly, too. I'm thinking that the old tale that all humans die during the change.... Are you all right, Jack?"

She nodded from her position. She should get used to having her head between her legs, because she'd been that way a lot lately. When the door to the kitchen opened, she didn't even have to look up to know it was Dylan. He had a scent now that she could smell, and it made her hungry. For him.

"Behave." She smiled at the thunder in his voice. She peeked up at him when he knelt down in front of her. "How you felling this morning? Any better?"

"If you say you're sorry again, I will hit you." He rubbed his nose, which looked good and had no sign of the earlier abuse she'd given it. "I feel great. For a panther, I guess. It worked."

"Yes. You're just like me." He leaned into her ear. "Except for a few more interesting parts that I would love to explore a bit more. You game to go out and shift?"

Shift. Was she ready? Yes. No. She had no ideam and sat up and looked around. What if she screwed it up? What if she couldn't go back? She wasn't terrified as much as scared shitless. He grinned at her and stood up.

"We're going outside for a while." He pulled her up off the chair. "Dad, could you please tell the others that we want to be alone until she gets used to this? She might have a few...issues."

His dad laughed and told him he'd make sure they weren't bothered. "Remember that there's still a mad man out there, and if you come across him, just have a snack or two on him. Vampire blood is something like a fine wine to us, or so I heard."

George was still laughing when they went out the door. She held Dylan's hand tightly, for some reason a little more afraid of this than she'd ever been going into a room blind. Jack told him that.

"You're going to do just fine. I've never heard of anyone having such...." He walked for a few feet before he continued. "When I bit you, I expected you to scream...was ready for it, actually. But you didn't make a sound. Not even a small whimper. I didn't...I fully expected that it hadn't worked."

"You were so afraid of hurting me that I didn't want you to think you had. I've been hurt before. Badly, as you know. But when I'm on an assignment I have to...." She, too, walked a little ways, thinking how to tell him how she felt. "There are times when it's not feasible, not even safe to acknowledge that you're in pain. If you do, then you're as good as dead. You don't last long in the field when you act like a big baby."

He seemed to understand and reached for her hand. When they were just on the inside of the stand of trees, she turned to him, just remembering to ask him something. She'd been in a hotel room when they had started her change. How did she end up back at Walker's house?

He flushed and looked away before answering. "I thought I'd killed you when you passed out. I called for Khan, then my dad. Mom came with them and started barking out orders like a drill sergeant on maneuvers. Had me terrified I'd disappointed her. She even had the hotel management doing what she wanted without a single question. We brought you back here so that you could rest, and I'd have a little more people around so that I wouldn't wake you every minute to ask you how you were feeling."

She laughed. She simply couldn't help it. Big bad Dylan Bowen, the calmest man she knew, had lost it. She was still smiling about it when he told her it was time. She realized then that they'd gone deep into the woods now. Nearly to the lake, he told her to strip, and he did the same.

"You have to trust me on this." She nodded. "Think of your panther. You know what I look like, so think of her in those terms. She'll come on her own, but you can't fight her. She's stronger and will come forth without hurting you if you let her."

The image of a sleek black cat came to her mind. She was huge, and when she snarled at her, Jack smiled back. She and her cat were going to butt heads, she knew. When she opened her eyes to ask Dylan what to do next, she was looking at him from a different perspective. And things looked…brighter. She looked up at her husband.

"You did it." She looked down at her body. "Christ, Jack, you look beautiful. And much bigger than Monica or Caitlynne."

She took offense to that and didn't know why she snarled at him. He laughed and finished taking off his clothes. She watched him as he stretched his arms over his head and shifted. Her breath caught when he was suddenly standing before her as his cat. He moved toward her slowly, and she backed up, suddenly not sure what he wanted from her.

"You run now and he'll chase you down. Don't move just yet. He wants to mark you with his fur." She lay down, trying her best not to run. *"Good girl. He's sort of hoping you'll be a good cat, but we both know that you won't be, will you?"*

She looked up at him, but spoke to Dylan. *"You are two different beings, aren't you? You're both cat and man, but not one in the same."*

"So will you be. I don't know why it happens that way, but I think it's actually easier that way for us. Two different—Christ, Jack come back here. He's going to be pissed."

She nipped at him and took off. Something inside of her said to run, and she ran for all she was worth. Leaping over logs and bushes, she felt the dirt beneath her paws and knew that the experience would only get better as she spent more time as a cat. Trees blurred by her, small animals ran. She was nearly to the other edge of the trees when she suddenly tumbled and rolled. He'd caught her.

His panther stood over her, and his giant paw held her down. He was panting hard, and she realized so was she. He looked furious, and she rubbed her head along his chest. His low growl made her wet, and she moved against him again.

"Stop that. Don't you know that he could hurt you?" He bit down on her shoulder when she tried to sit up. *"Christ, you scared us both. What were you thinking?"*

"I want you, Dylan, both of you." He growled low, and her body recognized that he wanted her, as well. Moving easier now that he'd gotten off her, she rolled to her belly and lay down. The big cat came up behind her and held her down again, but she knew this was different. This was his way of dominating her rather than simply wanting to keep her safe and near him. When he pushed her shoulders down to the ground, she raised her ass up to meet him.

"You're a virgin in this form. You won't like him taking you so hard." She moved against him again. *"You're going to make him pissy. But you don't care, do you?"*

She didn't. She wanted him, and they both knew it. When he snarled at her, loudly near her ear, she snarled back. Jack could hear Dylan's laughter, and when his cat bit her hard, she snarled again. But then he entered her, and she forgot to be mad.

His cock filled her, the pain short and sharp. She forgot about it almost as soon as it hurt. He snarled again when she moved, but he was just going to have to get over it because she needed more. The harder he slammed into her, his balls banging against her, she tightened, knowing that she was going to come as soon as he did. When he threw back his head and snarled, she came with him; his cum spilling from him made her come hard and long, much longer than she'd thought possible. Then she was being rolled to her back. Dylan, the man, looked down at her.

"Shift. For Christ's sake, shift. I need to fuck you." She didn't know what he meant but felt her body slide, and she looked back at him as a woman.

Dylan lifted her legs to his shoulders and entered her. His cock felt huge compared to that of the cat, and she cried out when he slammed into her again and again. When he leaned forward, her legs nearly to her chest, she felt the difference immediately. He was deeper than he'd ever been, thicker and harder, too. He looked into her eyes as he shifted around, letting her legs fall open around him. Lifting them to wrap around him, he moaned deeply. When he leaned his head down, she thought he was going to bite her, and she offered him her throat, her body tensing for the pain, but he only nuzzled her neck and moaned. But his offered throat was there for her.

Licking him, his pulse pounding at his vein, she felt her teeth shift, change in her mouth. Moaning, she licked again, tasting his scent on her tongue. He tasted spicy and hot. His sweat tingled on her tongue and wanted more of him.

"Bite me, Jack. Mark me. When you sink your teeth into me, you shake your head to leave a scar." He shifted again, and when he hit her sweet spot, she cried out her release and sank her teeth deeply.

Blood filled her mouth, and she swallowed. Heat filled her body, and she came again, coming so hard this time that she wanted to faint from it. Jerking her head hard, she tore at his flesh. More blood filled her mouth as he shouted out his own release. Even as he came, she still bit him, knowing that marking him was what would keep her from killing another female if they touched what was hers.

She licked the wound closed, the pink flesh already shaping into a scar...teeth marks that would be small, but would hold a great deal of meaning to anyone who saw them. Rolling him to his back, she pulled him up so that she was sitting on his lap, her legs wrapped around him.

He held her hips while she rode him slowly. His mouth danced across her breasts one at a time while she curled her fingers into his hair and held him to her. She moved over him, feeling the buildup again, and lifted his head so that she could take his mouth. Her climax poured over her softly as she held him, her body worn out and completely sated. Laying her head on his shoulder, she giggled at him. He pulled her head back and looked at her.

"Do you have any idea how much sex I had before I met you? Maybe four times in the last ten years." He bit her shoulder. "And now look. I'm in the woods with my husband, who I've not just had sex with twice, but once as a big fucking panther. Life couldn't get any better than this."

He rolled her to her back again, sliding easily in and out of her. "Oh, I don't know about that. I could bring you to a screaming climax a couple more times just to make it worth your while if you'd like."

He kissed her gently on the mouth, and she moaned. He continued to tease her by bringing her nearly to peak, then bringing her slowly down. She was ready to bash his brains in when she shifted beneath him. He touched her deeply, hitting something so carnal inside of her that she stiffened. It only lasted a second or two, but it took her breath away, made her arch up and grab him, for she feared that she was going to shatter at any second.

The climax roared from her. Not only did she scream, but she screamed over and over, telling him to stop, yet to give it all to her. When he finally came again, his body slamming into her hard, she came with him, this time begging him to stop, she couldn't take any more. When he dropped over her, she lay there without the strength to even lift her arms. This was the way life should be. She was smiling when she closed her eyes, rolling over with him. Spreading her body over his, she nuzzled into his chest and fell asleep.

Chapter Fifteen

Lucius watched the man and woman for three blocks, knowing that he was going to get what he wanted. And the girl that was with him was going to make things so much easier for him. Lucius was waiting for the perfect moment to take the man when another man, larger and taller, walked up behind them as they continued down the street. No matter, he was going to get his man, and she was going to give him what he wanted.

The opportunity was nearly lost when they stopped for several minutes in front of a store. If they went in, which was what Lucius was afraid of, he'd miss them. The sun was rising, and no matter what, he had to be back to the hotel before then or die. When they moved down the sidewalk, Lucius felt his first stirrings of the sun. It was coming now.

Materializing behind the younger man, he grabbed him. He opened his mouth to tell the girl his demands, but she turned suddenly, pushing the larger panther to the sidewalk. His arm exploded in pain. The smell of gunpowder was sharp in the air, and it burned his nose. Lucius reached for her, intending to take her with him, as well, or at the very least to kill her. She dodged him not once but twice. She moved quickly, her body fast and lethal as she hit him in his belly and throat with her small fist. When the man on the sidewalk rose, he didn't pull the girl back as he should have, but stepped back out of her way while she beat on him. He snarled at them and nearly lost his grip on the boy when the man reached out and grabbed his throat suddenly.

He was going to make them pay, but he had to leave now. He vowed to make them pay for what they'd done…make all of them pay for it. Even as he moved back to the hotel room he was growing weaker. The man in his arms, sleeping now that he'd put him under compulsion to rest, was growing nearly too much for him to hold. He put him in one of the chairs and moved to the ties he'd bought to tie him down.

Moving slowly, his body losing blood and growing weaker by the minute, he tied the boy down. He'd learned that they couldn't shift with the ties of plastic around their wrists and legs so tight. He didn't remember if he'd ever heard why not, but he didn't care so long as it worked. Lifting up the boy's head, he put a gag in his mouth and noticed the blood on his cheek. He had the overwhelming need to run from it and settled back on the bed to watch it flow from the cut there.

"I'm exhausted. Too tired is all. There is no reason at all that I would be afraid of his blood." Startled at the sound of his own voice yet comforted by it, Lucius moved to the head of the bed. "I will take care of you when I am rested. You'll be a good boy and stay put, or I'll simply tear out your throat."

Lucius again had the feeling that the boy's blood would harm him and staggered to the bathroom to look at his wound. He couldn't believe that the bitch had shot him, and that she'd done it so quickly. He wondered if she heard him or felt him, and decided that it was just his exhaustion talking again. A human, a female one at that, would not be able to detect a vampire, especially one as old as him.

She'd gotten him in the shoulder. The wound had stopped bleeding, but it still hurt. He washed at it gently, not wanting to make it bleed again, and thought of the girl and the man. He wondered now if she'd be so callus or so cold and uncaring that she'd not bring him Small and the things she had on him. He frowned at his reflection and tried to think why this one person, a person so beneath him, would cause him so much trouble. Throwing the rag on the floor, he stomped to the bedroom and looked at the male.

He was younger than the girl. Perhaps five years younger, but he was big. His scent was that of a full-blooded panther, and Lucius's mouth watered for a taste of him, even if it would only be a small one. But he still had that fear. Jerking the boy's head up by his hair, he slapped him hard. Blood already on his cheek now mingled with fresh blood from his mouth and nose. Feeling better, he went to the bed to lie down. He was closing his eyes when he felt the first touch of his mind.

Sitting up quickly, forgetting about the heaviness of his body, he looked around the room. Someone had to be close to him or he'd not be able to feel him. When the voice sounded, he had no idea of the sex of the person but had an uncontrollable urge to run and hide. He just knew it was the girl. But it wasn't, and his relief was so profound that he nearly missed the man's words.

"My name is Dylan Bowen, and you have my brother." There was a pause, long and full of shared feelings before the man continued. *"You want to fuck with me and mine, then you bring it on, buddy. I'll eat you for dinner. And you harm one hair on his head, and there will be nothing to keep me from staking you to the ground and pissing on your body as you go up in flames."*

Lucius believed him and shivered. But there was no way that this man, any man no matter what the species, was going to take him down. He knew that as surely as he was sitting there. Straightening up on the bed, Lucius looked at the boy in front of him. He glared at the panther in front of him and wished he had a reason why the thought of drinking from him, feeding from him, terrified him so. But he didn't want the man to know that.

"You think there is a reason for you to believe that I've not already dined on him?" The man laughed. *"You have that bitch of a female come to me and bring me Small. I want what she has on him, as well. All of it. You'll tell her that she will come to me at the front of the building where she lives at dusk, and to come alone. If I feel one person there that shouldn't be, I will do as I said. If she does not bring me what I want, I will kill this being that I have taken from her. I will rip his throat out and feast upon his blood."*

The man's laughter seemed to rattle in his mind and over his skin. Lucius was confused, not knowing if he cared so little for this panther or that he was as cold as the woman. Lucius wondered if the man might have been a good man to have on his side when he realized that he could no longer move his legs, the daylight taking his strength.

"She said to tell you that you'd better be there. She also said to tell you that Small won't get you what you want, but she will give you what you deserve." The laughter again. *"I'm thinking you might have fucked with the wrong woman when you messed with my wife."*

Lucius laid down his body, slowly shutting down, but his mind hadn't yet. She was coming for him. No, that wasn't right. She was going to bring him what he wanted, needed to make his plan work. He was going to get the man who would help him be rich beyond what he'd ever been. Closing his eyes again, he wondered about her. She was going to be difficult and thought that she might just be cocky enough to harm him. But he knew that she'd never kill him. It would be impossible for one female human to kill one such as him.

His last thought was of her. Her face was beautiful, her body strong and full of spark. Frowning as he tried to quiet his mind, he worried that she was more than he thought she was. More than he'd ever encountered in female or male.

~~~

She watched Dylan, waiting for him to go off on her as the others were doing. Well, they weren't so much yelling at her, but they were upset. The monster had Reed. When Dylan put his fingers in his mouth and whistled, everyone in the room stopped and looked at him.

"I haven't heard you do that in an age. Who is it that taught that to you?" His dad said with a laugh, then sat down, continuing to chuckle. "Did you know that he could whistle so that no matter how many people were around us we'd know it was Dylan?"

"No one taught me. I'm naturally talented that way." Dylan stood up and pulled Jack into his arms. "You guys are upsetting Jack. She can't tell us how she's going to get Reed out if we have her pissy with us. She might just leave the lot of us on our own and go get him herself. Foolhardy that would be, now wouldn't it, love?"

"I should go alone." He shook his head. "I didn't say I was, I just said I should. You don't have the training I do, and even if you did, it's my fault the guy has him."

"How on earth do you figure that?" Caitlynne stood up as well with her hands on her hips. "You do know that you're not the only one here that can carry a gun? And last time I looked, we're all family here, and we work together. You slowed him down by shooting him, kept him from taking all of you. I think what you did was brave. Stupid but brave."

Jack snorted before speaking. "You wouldn't know how to take orders from someone if you knew it was the only way to get out of something. And as for the rest of you, I've never seen a bigger bunch of bossy people in my life. But I understand the family part. Sometimes. But I should have made Reed stay at the house where I knew it was safe."

Reed had met her downtown. She needed to get a few things, clothes mostly, and he said that he knew of a great shop on Pennsylvania. She knew he carried, and that he'd been trained a little on how to defend himself, but this guy played a different ballgame than any of them were used to.

"You'll get him back to us. We all will." Corrine patted her on the shoulder. "You're going to have to learn to see yourself as a part of our family, too, dear. If you don't, then I think Monica and Caitlynne will have a little talk with you. You know how they are…bossy women just like someone else I know."

They settled down to plan. Khan kept trying to contact his brother, but couldn't. He said that the connection was there, meaning he wasn't dead. Jack was relieved to hear that. She looked up when Caitlynne came into the study with them all. She didn't look like she was bringing good news.

"They found a body at the Gentleman's Hotel on Seventh an hour ago. It took them until now to verify who it was. Kirby Mann was murdered. They're saying a wild animal did it." She sat down and tossed a file on the desk. "I got that twenty minutes ago, and I was reading it when the call came in. It's from Mann. I suppose it could be called his last will and testament. He confessed to every crime he ever committed all the way back to grade school. He even confessed to being a part of the treason that Small and Jackson were in on."

"Do you suppose he knew that he was going to be dead soon and wanted to meet his maker with a clean slate?" Caitlynne shrugged at her question. "Where are his wife and daughter? They weren't there, were they?"

"No, just him. And I don't know where they are. I sent a car to the house, and there was no answer. Maid said that the missus and the daughter had gone on vacation. She didn't know where Mann had gone. She said that there had been no calls, either." Caitlynne laughed. "I don't think he was well-liked by his staff. They hinted that if he didn't come back, they wouldn't lose any sleep over it."

Jack could believe that. He treated his secretary with less respect than he treated her, and that was pretty bad. When she looked at the file, she flipped to the back pages and stood up. He mentioned Lucius.

"They're dead. Sally and Karrie, he believes, are dead. He sent them away so they might be safe, and Lucius took them. Mann thinks he killed them as soon as he took them. He said that...." She flipped back several pages to when he first mentioned him. "Apparently, Lucius showed up when his wife was dying some years ago. Right after they'd found out about the baby. Lucius gave her his blood and took hers. That explains how he was able to find them, I guess."

"So he saves his wife and daughter, and what? Owes him for the rest of his life?" Jack nodded at Khan and said that he'd been owned by Lucius since. "Why didn't he just let someone know what was going on?"

"Because he was getting everything he wanted by helping out the blood sucker." Jack sat down as she continued reading. "Listen to this. 'Lucius calls me human. I don't think he's ever said my name in all this time. I believe we're all just cattle to him. But he does seem to have a weakness. His temper gets the better of him every time.' A temper could work in our favor."

Dylan started to shake his head, but Caitlynne agreed with her. "Yes. Because we both know that pissed-off people make huge mistakes. Do you have a plan?"

She did, but she thought that if she told them they'd be pissed, too. She simply shook her head. Jack wanted to stew on it just a little longer before she told them. But they had less than ten hours until sunset and getting Reed back. Then she looked at the computer.

"Did Reed have his cell phone on him when he left the office?" No one knew for sure. He was forever leaving it behind when he left work. Picking up a phone, she asked for his number and dialed it while calling for Sebastian or Marc to help her. She had a feeling that they might be able to find him this way.

Marc went to his office to work with the equipment he had there. "When you call it, I'll be able to pinpoint where he is to within a few hundred feet. If he's turned off his phone, then it will be considerably more than that."

She knew that but wanted to try anyway. It rang a total of eight times before going to voicemail. She let the mailbox cut her off before hanging up, then called Marc back. He was laughing, he was so excited.

"You want a job working for me, you can have it. We know where he is. He's at the Hotel Monaco in the Penn Quarter. I'm not sure what floor or even room number, but that's where Reed's phone is coming from."

She hung up and looked at the people in the room. Marc was coming back, but she doubted she'd have any problems with him. These people, however, were going to be hard to convince.

"I know where he is." Relief settled over the room, and she looked at Dylan. "I can get him out of the room now before the vampire wakes, but we have to be ready for him to be able to defend himself, too."

"What is it you have to do?" Dylan smiled at her. "You know what has to be done, so simply tell us, and we'll stand where you need us."

Before anyone could say anything, Khan spoke. "She's right. And so is Dylan. If she's sure she can get him out, I think we should do what she says. Unless someone else has a better plan than the one she's going to tell us, then we're ready to help."

"You're not going to like this, but it's all I have." She pulled up the hotel on the computer and looked at the rooms. "He's more than likely going to be holding Reed in the same room with him. If that's the case, then he's going to be tied to something, more than likely a chair. Is there any reason why he won't be able to shift if we need him to heal or something?"

"If there are cuffs or even plastic ties at his wrists and legs and they're too tight, then they will sever his hands and feet off if he shifts because his cat is much bigger than his human. Then there's the added problem that if he's tied to something heavy and the bonds don't break, then he's going to be tethered to it." She nodded at Khan, then looked at Dylan.

"If I asked you to stay here, would you?" He smiled, and she had her answer. "Yeah, I thought so. But when we go in, you'll do as I say when I say it? All of you?"

She had some hesitations, but George said that if any of them disagreed, he'd have to kick their ass. She believed him, and apparently so did the others. She had their promise before she launched into the plan.

"We're going to have to go in and pull Reed out. If what you say about being put to sleep by the vampire is true, then he won't be able to wake until he's far enough away from his spell or the vamp is dead. I want to make sure that the Mann's are really dead before I kill him. I don't know if he has them stashed somewhere, and I don't want to find them months later."

Everyone agreed, but Sebastian posed a question. "Then what do we do? There are as many ways to kill a vampire as there are snowflakes. How do we know which one will work?"

Jack agreed with him. It was hard to know what would work and what was Hollywood hype. She laid her gun on the table and then her knife, and had a feeling that they'd be useless, and told them so. They were both your run-of-the-mill Glock and knife. She wondered aloud what to take with them.

"Once he wakes, he's going to go after me with everything he has. Do I fill these with silver and hope they work on him like they did on the wolves? I doubt a cross would do me much good, other than something to pray to if he starts to look like he might win." Picking up the gun, she rolled her wrist, testing the weight as she continued. "We can't take it all, but we need something. I'm for less is better normally, but in this situation I'm thinking I might have enough time to try two, maybe three things before he rips my head off."

"You'll have me and the gun." Dylan took the gun from her. "My cat and yours as well. That gives you four. What else?"

She looked around the room and thought of all the shit she'd seen in the movies when she'd been able to catch one.

What had done the most damage and had taken out the most vampires? She looked at the crossed swords over the mantel.

"Those real?" Walker looked at them, then at her, grinning. "If I could take off his head, I'm pretty sure that'd stop him for a while, if not forever."

She and Dylan went to the hotel on his bike. He'd gone to the garage with her, and when he skirted around the bike to the truck, she asked him if they could go on it. She rode on the back of it wrapped around his body and felt the air rush around them. The others were coming in the cars.

Caitlynne went in first and talked with the manager. Dylan and she stood nearby. The manager said that there was no one in the hotel by the name of Lucius. They had no last name, so, starting at the top, they were going to go door to door and ask everyone to leave. Monica had said to use the story of an electrical problem because it would cause less panic. *Yeah*, Jack thought, *telling them that a big vampire was about to be killed by a bunch of werepanthers would be hard to swallow*. As soon as they got off the elevator, the scent of blood burned her nostrils, and she looked at Dylan.

"It's not fresh, but it is panther." He touched her mind and sent her his love. *"You can do this, I know you can."*

Going to the only door on the floor, she leaned her head against it. There were no sounds coming from inside, so she used the passkey to get into the room. The smell there was stronger, much stronger than she'd found in the hall. Moving to the two rooms, she went to the one to the back of the hotel suite and opened the door quietly, then shut it again when she saw how dark it was.

"You sure you can see him?" Dylan had been joined by Khan, and they both nodded. "Go in and get him out then. Don't make a sound. If you wake him before I get in there, shift and run like hell."

177

Dylan pulled her to him and kissed her. She felt his desperation, and she knew that he'd felt hers. Closing the room's curtains, they went back to the bedroom door and opened it. Someone was sitting in a chair, slumped over. She went in first, Then they each took an arm to the chair and picked him up and took him out of the room without a sound. She moved out of the room with them and watched as Walker checked him out. With a short nod, Khan and Walker took Reed out of the room and to the elevator. She picked up a chair similar to the one Reed had been in.

"You ready?" She nodded as he handed her the swords. When he shifted and moved into the room in front of her, she closed the door behind them. They were caged with a monster and hoped to Christ they could get out again.

Chapter Sixteen

Dylan watched her. She sat in the chair as if she had not a care in the world. He, however, was terrified out of his mind. They were actually going to question a vampire in his own den, then kill him. He looked out the window and knew that the sun was going down. Only a couple of hours to go now before Lucius woke. Dylan felt her touch his mind and waited for her to tell him that she'd made a mistake in doing this, hoping that was what she would say.

"When I was nineteen, I was a sophomore in college and this man approached me. He said that he had a job for me to do. He said that if I did it and I lived he had a job for me and that the firm he worked for would pay my student loans and help me get set up in a nicer apartment. Would have had to have been better, I was living in my friend's garage at the time."

He lay down and tried to relax to the sound of her voice. *"What did he want you to do? I'm assuming that he wanted you to do something you were good at."*

She laughed, and he found himself smiling. He knew that she was talking to him to calm him. He didn't want her there, but he also knew that of all the people he knew, she was the best suited for his job.

"No, not back then anyway. I was trying my best to go on the straight and narrow. I'd never killed anyone before that, but he knew my background and everything else about me, including my record. He said that this would be my first test of many." She laughed through their link. *"It was a test all right. I was arrested when I went to the police to report him."*

He waited for her to continue, knowing that it would be a good one. When she shifted on the chair, he tensed, waiting for the vampire on the bed to rise. But when she continued with her story, he relaxed again.

"That was the test, you see. He'd given me all the information and the gun I needed to carry out the job. I was to go into a house, kill the man on the bed, and leave without setting off any of the alarms. When I went to the police and told them my side of the story, I was arrested, and when he found out, he had them put me in a cell. He showed up an hour later." She was quiet for a little while. *"They put me in this small room with a mirror. I'd done enough stupid stuff in my short life as a criminal that I knew there was someone on the other side, so I sat there and closed my eyes. When someone kicked my chair out from under me, I leapt up, tossed the man to the floor, and put his gun to his head. Do you know what he did?"*

Dylan laughed when she did. *"He kicked your ass. Or did he laugh at you? I'm guessing that he was a cop or something like that. Who was he?"* Dylan would bet that the younger Jack was much more volatile than this one.

"His name was Wilton Guzman and yes, he was something of a cop. He was an agent for the CIA, and they were doing some recruiting in the area, and my foster father had told him about me. He told me if I let him up without hurting him, he'd have something to offer me. Guzman told me that if I could get into the house just like he told me to and

get out, he'd not press charges for me assaulting an agent for the United States government." She laughed again. *"I knew the neighborhood and the house, you see, so I had a little information about where he wanted me to go. I'd even gone there before going to the police just to see where it was. But this time I had to get in and had to get out. He wasn't going to help me if I got caught, either, he said."*

Moving closer to her when she moved her arm to her lap, he put his head close enough so that she could pet him from his position on the floor. Dylan doubted that she realized what she was doing so lost in thought, but he did. And it was all he could do not to purr loudly at her. She continued with her story while she stroked his fur.

"The house was a large two-story that had lots of windows and a great deal of landscaping around them. I'd broken into houses before to find a place to sleep sometimes and had learned to be careful. Dogs, wild ones, are very territorial and have no problem running you from what they considered theirs. I'd spent plenty of nights on the cold ground while a stupid mutt lay in a dry building. Also, I had to be careful of some homeless people. They can be mean when you cross their path." Dylan had known that she had lived a less than perfect life, but not this badly. *"Anyway, I had dressed all in black and wore a mask over my face, and entered the yard to the back of the property then got down on my belly to move in. I saw three men in the yard and slid past them without any trouble. When I got to the house, I knew there was a motion sensor light in the backyard, so I avoided it by going to the front of the house."* She paused in her petting and he waited. She seemed to have gotten lost for a few seconds in a memory and it appeared to be a good one from her smile. He waited for her to continue.

"They thought I'd come in from the rear for whatever reason. But they were no less ready for me in the front, I suppose. The light to the alarm system was off, but I figured that was a trick and didn't assume it was off, just the light had been disabled. I saw that there was a small window in the basement, so I went there. It was small, but back then as college student without money, so was I. Cutting through the screen to the basement, I was able to drop to the floor about an hour before sunset so the basement was dark and empty.

"The house was dead quiet, but I'd lived in an older house like this one and knew that steps creaked and walls settled, so I was able to tell footstep sounds above me as opposed to the ones the house made. Going to the stairs, I nearly fell down them when I slipped on a pile of dirty laundry sitting at the bottom of an opening. As I nearly tumbled, I hit an opening above my head and grabbed on. It was the laundry chute. I found a ladder and moved under it. As I stood up to stand in the opening, I heard someone speaking softly on the other side, so I stilled for a few moments. It was at my height to see into the bathroom, and I could see that the room was empty of anyone. Climbing up the shaft was easy. There were slates there that had been left behind when the thing had been the only way into the crawlspace years ago, I was told. As soon as I was in the main part of the house, I went to the kitchen." She laughed as she continued. *"Someone had been having a snack and had left it there for me to take. So I took the jar of peanut butter off the counter and ate the sandwich. I wrote the person a thank-you note with the pen and paper on the counter. Going back out was easy. As I went back to the laundry shaft, I still hadn't heard anything on this level, but there was someone on the stairs either going up or down. I couldn't tell. I crawled back down it, finished my dinner, and was out the window*

again before the house exploded in light. They caught me in the yard."

When she didn't finish, he thought how disappointed she must have been. To have worked so hard to get into the house and only to have failed when she came back out. He wondered if she ever regretted taking the sandwich that more than likely had gotten her caught. But he knew that she would find that to be her prize and smiled.

"So you failed. Christ, that must have hurt after all that work." She smiled down at him and shook her head. *"They didn't arrest you, did they? I hope to Christ not. That would be so unfair of them after telling you to break in."*

"I only had to get in the house and out. I did that. The man I stole the sandwich from wasn't all that happy with me, but he did say he'd been impressed. He had only stepped out for less than a minute, and when he'd returned, he knew that I'd gotten in somehow. He said if not for that, I might have made it all the way back the way I came. He said that the note was something that he'd keep for a very long time, and use it to remind himself there was more than one way into a house and back out again. I think he still has it in his office. He calls me occasionally when he wants to talk about it."

Dylan laughed. He couldn't help it. She'd out-smarted them all, and ate dinner, too. He wanted to ask her if she'd gotten the job but realized that she had, sort of. She'd been recruited, but not to where she'd thought she was going. He was sad for her about that and knew that Caitlynne was working to get Jack onto her team.

He moved when she straightened. He heard the heart start to beat slowly and knew that the vampire was waking. As he to the position on the floor nearest the bed in the event she needed him, she sat in the chair and didn't move.

~~~

Lucius could smell the cat as soon as he woke up. It had startled him for a few seconds, wondering how a cat had gotten into his room. Then he remembered the boy he'd taken and settled down. He waited before moving, knowing that the young panther would still be asleep. Stretching, he moved so that his back was to the headboard and reached over and turned on the light. He looked back toward the boy and nearly cried out when he saw the woman sitting where he'd left his prey. She waved at him.

"Good evening, Lucius. I do hope you slept well. Also, did you know that your heart doesn't beat when you sleep? And when the sun starts to go down, it starts working again? Slow at first, but it picks up speed the lower the sun gets." She shrugged. "Just an observation."

He looked around the room and could see that the panther was gone. When he looked back at her, he saw that there was a gun in her hands, and he could smell the silver from where he sat. He started to move but stopped when she cleared her throat and shook her head at him.

"Unless you want me to shoot you now instead of later, I would suggest that you sit still. I'd like to ask you a few questions." She picked up a sheet of paper off her lap. "The first one is what did you need Small for, and—"

"What are you doing here? You were not invited here. I told you I'd meet you in front of your house. I demand that you go there now and I shall meet you there." He started to move again, and she fired a bullet into the headboard not an inch from his head. "You nearly shot me."

"I know, damn it. If you hadn't moved when you did, I would have, too. Next time, if you wouldn't mind not moving around so much, I'll see if I can get a clear shot." He looked at her, stunned. She was actually telling him how to behave so she could shoot him. He started to rise again when she lifted the gun. He simply refused to deal with one such as her.

"I would like for you to leave now." He heard what he was saying and had a hard time believing it himself. He didn't really expect her to leave, but maybe she was just stupid enough to do as he told her. Apparently not.

"I have a question or two that I'd like to ask you before we go. The first one is about the Manns, Sally and Karrie. Where are they?" He looked at her, confused. "You called her husband Kirby 'human' she said. Or is that what you call all of us, 'human'?"

"You're all barely that to me. Cattle are what I would label you. Just like all the other stupid, mindless animals that do little more than wander around the field eating grass and other things. On occasion, they give milk to supply you other mindless animal's things like cheese and milk, byproducts that make them fat and lazier. All of you should be put into pens and fed once a day, then slaughtered when you serve your purpose."

"So from that I can assume you don't like us. Well, buddy, I don't care much for you taking my family from me, either. Do you even care that we were having a good time until you came along and messed it up? I don't shop often, but when I do, I like it to go smoothly." She picked up the paper again. "Okay now, where are the human's Sally Mann and her daughter Karrie Mann? By the way, bang up job on killing Kirby. I think they'll be picking pieces of him out of that room for years to come." He nodded at her compliment. He'd been angry at the human, but he had brought it all on himself. He still thought of that machine he'd been messing with, but doubted that it had been anything more than a toy to entertain him. But his good feeling at what she'd said was short lived when she spoke again.

"Of course, he did send us all a confession of everything you and he had been up to for all this time. The two of you were very busy little beavers, weren't you? I mean, the list is long and very helpful. You had him by the balls, didn't you?"

"I have no idea what you're going on about. I don't know any Mann person any more than I know anyone else you've spoken about. And I most assuredly don't want anything more to do with you. Go away." Her laughter made him want to get up and slap her until her neck snapped. But every time he moved she would point that gun at his chest, and he knew she'd have him dead before he was able to get across the room.

A movement to his right had him moving farther to the opposite side of the bed. A large panther, much bigger than any other one he'd seen, was sitting there licking his paws. When the cat leapt up on the bed, Lucius started to move. Then the girl cleared her throat. He was trapped for now.

"Okay, we're going to do this again. Where are Sally and Karrie Mann, wife and daughter of Kirby Mann, the person you killed in a hotel room several days ago?" Her voice had grown hard and no longer full of humor. He knew she was getting mad at him, but he didn't care. He was going to kill her soon enough.

Lucius knew he had two choices, and neither of them sounded like he would make it out in one piece. She wouldn't be able to kill him—of that he was fairly certain—but she would hurt him. One plan was that he tried to materialize behind the girl, kill her, and deal with the panther while he did so, or he could let her take him before the council. He wasn't thrilled with either of those ideas because he knew that he was wanted for a great many crimes, more than the girl knew about, that would get him killed by them. He watched her sit there as if she had not one care in the world. Lucius made his move.

He was behind the girl before the cat moved. When Lucius looked at the headboard where his head had been only seconds before, he was glad that he'd been gone when the cat moved. The gouges left by his massive paw tore into the wood at least three inches deep and a foot long. His head would have been severed from his body in seconds had he been the slightest bit slower.

Holding her head back with a handful of her hair and a knife he'd taken from one of his victims at her throat, he looked at her. He knew the cat wouldn't move, not when he had her like this. He smiled down at her, and she winked at him. He hated when she did that and thought that she knew it. He shook her head hard.

"Are you so stupid that you don't realize what I could and will do to you? You are nothing to my strength and age, you ignorant female." The cat snarled at him. "Tell him to be quiet or I'll tear your throat out."

"No." He looked at the cat, then at her again. Was she serious? Apparently so. The cat jumped off the bed and sat at her legs. When he laid his head on her, Lucius knew that he was her mate.

"So you've found yourself a panther to fuck. Good for you. I do hope that you've enjoyed him. When I'm through with you, he'll run from you every time you enter the room. That is if I let you live. Which I don't think is going to happen for you." He yanked her head back harder and looked at the pulse beating slowly.

"You think that I'm afraid of you, don't you." He nodded, confused by her lack of fear. "You're the one who should be afraid. I mean, what kind of idiot lets a mere slip of a girl get into his room with a pissed off panther? Not to mention take what you stole from her in the first place. You're the ignorant one, you fuck-tard."

He glanced at the panther, which hadn't moved. He looked...Lucius thought he looked bored, and when he closed his eyes, Lucius was sure he'd fallen asleep. He watched her hand move toward the cat's head and begin to rub it. When the cat began to purr loudly, Lucius wanted to scream.

"You are trying my patience." He felt spittle drip from his mouth. He wasn't sure what to do with her, or the cat. Moving the knife deeper into her flesh, he watched as a small drop of blood beaded up on the fresh wound. Fear of her suddenly tripled.

"You really think I would come in here without a plan? You think that because I'm a girl that I would come in here so ill prepared that I'd let you take me so easily?" She smiled at him and he felt shivers, cold and frightening, run down his spine. "Cut me again and I'll kill you."

Her voice had been so low, so full of promise, that he knew she would do just as she said she would. Lucius looked at the cat and saw that he was no longer sleeping but looking at him as well. In that second, he knew he wasn't leaving this room.

"If I tell you where they are, will you let me go?" She laughed, hardy and with a great deal of humor. "I will tell you if you let me go."

Her hand snaked out and grabbed his, the one with the knife, and she jerked him around so quickly that he had no choice but to follow the flow. As soon as his back was to the floor, she was over him, his knife at his own throat, and she was holding it.

"I know where they are. You had your manservant take them away when there was nothing much left of them but a shell. You tore out the daughter's throat without feeding from her, because you were sick of her whining. The mother you enjoyed. Her blood was spiked with fear and anger. You killed them not an hour after you snatched them from their hotel the first day of their vacation."

"There is no way that you would know that." But there was, and she did know it, knew it all. "I demand that you give me my due. I wish to be brought before the council of my kind. I will stand before them in trial and not hunted and killed by you."

She leaned down to him, the knife deep into his skin, yet not breaking it. She looked calm, and for whatever reason, that frightened him more. The woman was mad, he realized. Mad as a hatter. When she kissed his forehead, he jerked from her, and the knife cut him. He didn't move when she pulled away.

"I'm your judge and your jury, you fucking asshole. And we've gotten all I want from you, thanks to my mate." The knife slid along his throat to his chest, where she paused. "I'm your executioner, too."

The knife plunged deep. He knew the exact moment it touched his heart. Pain tore through him, and he worked quickly to repair the damage. It wasn't silver, so he may survive, he thought. When she stood up off him, he grabbed at his chest, using his energy to stop the flow of blood and work at closing off the wound. Closing his eyes, he tried to make it look as if he was dying. Then there was sharpness at this throat.

She stood over him, a sword in her hands. He watched her pull it from his neck to a full arch above her body. He couldn't move, couldn't do anything as his energy level was too low from loss of blood. The silver blade came around, a work of beauty in the way that she and the sword seemed to be one. When it sliced though his neck, he had seconds to appreciate her strength and her aim. Few could have taken a head from a full-grown man as smoothly as she'd done.

Chapter Seventeen

Jack sat on the deck of her home and watched the river flow past. She'd been out there since the first rays of the sun had touched the mountain. The unopened box that the wizard had given them was under the chair where she sat. She looked up when the door opened behind her and Dylan stepped out.

"You couldn't sleep?" She shook her head. "I'm worried about you. I thought that coming here would be good for you. You've not slept a whole night in over a week."

She'd been sleeping but not restfully. She kept playing over and over in her head the way that the vampire had died. She shivered when she remembered him falling apart, his skin becoming hard and brittle as he—

"Stop that." She looked at Dylan when he sat near her. "You can't keep thinking about it. You saved us and my brother. Reed said he tried to talk to you about it again yesterday."

"I'm not ready yet." She kicked the box and leaned over to pick it up. "This came today. Khan sent it, I think. That man has the worst handwriting I've ever seen. And how on earth did he know the address here? I don't even know it."

"I called the post office and asked them. They said they have some of your mail there and asked if we were going to put up a mail box. I told them I didn't know but we'd come in and get the mail today." She nodded.

"I don't want to open it. The box…I don't want to open it. What if it's stuff that would be from the vampire? I don't want to…." She looked at the fast moving river again. "I have killed before, but when I took his life, I took it without him being able to fight back. I murdered him."

She knew that he was aware of the dreams. It would be hard for him not to know since they slept together every night. She also knew that he was trying to help her, and she loved him for it. But she had killed a man, killed him when he'd had no way to defend himself. She looked over when Dylan picked up the box.

He tore at the packaging and then sat there for several seconds with the smallish chest on his lap. She knew it was heavy; when the postman handed it to her she knew that something more had been added, a great deal more. Jack wondered if Khan had sent something else with it, but all that was there were the chest and the wrapping. Dylan stood up.

"Come into the house with me. I'll open it, and you can fix us breakfast." She took his hand when he offered it. "I would love some waffles. The kind you made the first night we were here. And ham. I love fried ham."

She went to the refrigerator and started taking out the things to make waffles, and he sat in the chair. The box sat there in front of him, and she tried to ignore it by changing the subject. She glanced at the calendar and asked him about school.

"When do you need to go back to class? I'm assuming you have to go in before school actually starts to do some things." He said he would, yes. "I don't even know what grade you teach."

"Fifth. I teach fifth grade and gym on Tuesdays all day. It's sort of nice. I get to know a great many of the kids I might not have being just a teacher. What are you going to do now?"

She had had offers to go back to work for Caitlynne, but she wasn't sure she could do that right now. She'd received a nice bonus for solving the case against the country when she'd figured out Mann's last two overseas accounts. And that money was still in an uncashed check with the one she'd gotten from the Vampire Council for taking care of Lucius. That check was considerably bigger. But until she cashed one or both of them she had to find a job.

"Your brother Marc offered me a job. He might have been kidding, but I was thinking of going into that line of work if he didn't want me." She tried not to think about that and moved on. "I could open my own investigating firm, something like he has. Monica said he's very good."

"He wasn't kidding when he offered you the job. He has asked me several times if you were ready to talk business yet." Dylan got up and started making a pot of tea for them. "My dad said that Mom misses you. I think he does more; you and he got along very well."

They had, too. He was funny and witty, just like she'd always dreamed of a dad being. He had texted her every day since they'd been there and had sent her pictures of the babies, all three of them, as well.

As they sat down to eat, she tried not to see the box. She thought about asking him to put it on the floor, but that would be like admitting that she was afraid of it. She looked at him when he laughed.

"I have been really good about not invading your mind. I've wanted to a great deal and have just been worried enough about you to do it anyway. But it's your face that gives you away sometimes. When you think you're alone or deep in thought, you have the most telling face." She started to get up and toss her plate in the sink when he stopped her. "We never have to open this box. Never. I don't care what's in it enough to force you to open it, any more than I care why he gave it to us. But he did."

"What if it's something from the vampire?" Once she said it she knew she had to tell him. "I'm terrified it's some sort of award for killing him. I don't want anything for killing him. Nothing at all. I murdered him because he'd taken Reed. I killed him because I didn't want him to hurt your family, my family. I cut off his head because I didn't want to have to look over my shoulder for the rest of my life."

"That does not make you a murderer. It makes you human. And had you not killed him, who else do you suppose he would have killed? My mother? My dad? Or even me? How long do you think the council would have been able to hold him before he escaped?" He pushed the box toward her. "We can take it to the river right now and toss it in. I don't want you to do anything that makes you uncomfortable."

"And the money?" He shrugged. "So if I told you that I want to shred the checks and not cash them, you'd be okay with that?"

"We didn't have it before, so not having it now makes no difference to me." He stood up and pulled her into his arms. "I have all I need right here, right now. I love you, very much, and will never leave you no matter what you decide."

He held her so tightly that she believed him. Burying her head in his chest, she felt the tears that she'd been hiding from for over a week start to flow. Before long she was sobbing and clinging to him. At some point, he picked her up and sat in the chair while she continued to cry. Exhausted, her body began to relax and ease. The last thing she remembered was being put to bed, and she rolled over and slept.

~~~

Dylan watched her sleep for a few minutes before he left the bedroom and went to the kitchen. He was cleaning up their leftovers when his cell phone rang. He smiled when he realized it was his dad.

"She bringing you home soon?" He laughed at his dad's greeting. "I can't say I miss you overly much, but your mother does. The girl, too. We're fixing to have a big family dinner when you and she get your bottoms here."

"She's sleeping." He heard his dad sigh. "I'm hoping that she'll sleep for a few hours. Then we'll talk some more."

"She still not sleeping, then?" He'd talked to his parents every day since they'd gotten there. "Poor thing. That girl has more guts and balls than most men I know of. Saved not just your brother, but you, too. I knew she was going to be good for you."

She was, too, and he glanced toward the bedroom. "Dad, what if she never learns to deal with this? What if this haunts her for the rest of her life? I don't want her to suffer because she feels like a failure."

"She's not a…. I want you to bring her here, to home. I'll have a good talk with her, and if that don't work, then I'll take her out to the woodshed. She'll see reason once she's had a taste of my switch." Dylan grinned.

There was no switch and never had been. The first time he'd been taken there he'd expected no less than having his legs bleeding for a month and that he'd need massive reconstructive surgery to put him back together. But what he'd done to him that day was much worse. His dad had told him how disappointed he'd been in his actions, and went on to point out that he'd let his mother down, as well. Dylan had never been back to the shed. He'd not been perfect, but one look from his dad, that look that told him he was getting close, was all it would take to straighten him around.

"I'll ask her if she's ready to come back. But I know why she loves it here. It's peaceful and homey." He looked around the kitchen after telling his dad he'd try to get her home in a few days and hanging up.

The cabinets were glass fronted and lighted from above. The table was huge in both size and weight. She'd made it from lumber that had been left over from building the house. The floor was quarried stone she'd had brought in and was heated from beneath. Jack had told him the first morning there that she'd never spent her money on clothes or anything else, and had sank everything she'd made into this place. It showed.

The living room/dining room had a stone fireplace in it that heated the house. Vents that were fed from the fireplace had been placed throughout the entire house. They heated the entire house without the need for ductwork. She said in the winter if she had a good fire going, she could get it up to nearly eighty degrees.

The bedroom was huge and had a view and a deck that was amazing. They'd left the door opened nightly to let in the fresh night air and the sounds of the forest. He had never slept better in his life than he had that first night. After that, he'd been too worried about her to do more than hold her while she tossed and turned. When he was finished washing up the dishes, he went to the bedroom again. She was still sleeping.

Stripping down, he crawled into the bed with her. She was warm and soft, but he tried not to hold her too tightly and wake her. As soon as he pulled the covers over them again, she rolled over and wrapped herself around him. He closed his eyes and decided to try and sleep while she did.

The room was dark when he woke. She was still sleeping, so he got up to go to the bathroom and wash up. He looked in the mirror and thought he looked rested…more so than he'd looked earlier. When he pulled his cell phone out of the drawer he'd been putting it in so as not to wake her, he was shocked to see he'd missed nine phone calls and a few dozen texts, all of them from his family. That's when he realized the date was different. They'd been asleep for well over twenty-four hours. Dylan went back to the bedroom to find her awake.

"Hi. How you doing?" She smiled at his question. "We must have needed this, because we've been in bed for a whole day and a half."

"No way. I haven't been sleeping well. That can't be right." He handed her his phone when he got back in the bed with her. "Are you sure this is right?"

"I know. I didn't believe it either, but I think it's right. I feel like it's right, too. I feel great." She lay back down, and he pulled her to him.

"I feel better, too." She stretched over him and his cock jerked. "Dylan, do you want to open the box now?"

He wanted to tell her later, that he wanted to open her now, but nodded. She got up and went to the kitchen, and returned with the box. She sat on the bed with her legs crossed and looked at it.

"It's probably nothing. I've been worrying about nothing." He asked her if she believed that. "No, but I know that I have to open it or it will eat me up inside."

She flipped up the small clasp and started to raise the lid. She reached for his hand and told him to help her as Jacob had told them to open it together. When the lid was back as far as it would go, they looked inside. On top was a letter.

"It's from Jacob." She opened it slowly. "He starts it with a thank you."

"Thank you so much for what you have done for everyone. Not just for your family but for all mankind, in the future as well as your own time. There have been many before you who have tried, but no one but you have succeeded.

"You'll find within this chest a great amount of wealth. Not just of the monetary kind, but of things you'll learn to treasure and hold. The money has been added to over the centuries by different wizards, as well as me, who had to hide to stay alive. We were fighting a losing war with Lucius long before he decided to take the White House. He has hunted our kind to near extinction.

"I would like to visit you again someday soon, but for now know that I will continue to watch over you all. I have a special fondness for panthers myself as I started my life as one before becoming a wizard. It was only after I changed that I realized how much I missed being able to run with a family.

"Good luck in all that you do. I hope that you will know that everything you did you did for the greatness of mankind. You have saved so many people, human and others, that you cannot know how indebted we will be to you forever. Sincerely, your friend Jacob."

Dylan dumped the contents of the box on the bed and looked at it, stunned. Jacob wasn't kidding when he said there was a great amount of wealth. There was enough in just stones that they could live off of for years...lifetimes...without ever spending it all. He picked up one of the larger rubies while Jack picked up the small thumb drives.

"I think this is big enough to buy us a country," he said. She laughed as she picked up another drive and handed it to him. "What is this? What do you suppose this means?"

She said she had no idea but got up to get her laptop. He picked up several more of the drives and they each said one word on them: tiger, panther, bear, and so on. There seemed to be a drive for each species of animals. When she sat down again he handed her the one that said panther. She brought up the file, and he looked over her lap at what was there.

"Oh my God, it's a list. A list of every panther known, as well as mates and children. Your family is here, as is my name and Monica's and Caitlynne's and their children." She moved the mouse more quickly now, then stopped. "This is a list of known abilities that each may have, as well as a list of things unique to them. What on earth do you suppose he gave this to us for?"

There was a small notation near his name, and he asked her to read it. He knew what it said before she started. Someone knew what he could do, as well as Monica. He was afraid.

"It says 'Special Ability: No boundaries. Dylan Bowen is able to read the mind of every being with a mind. Animals as well as human. He will pass this on to his children and them on to theirs. He is to be saved at all costs." She looked at him. "Dylan, what does he mean that you should be saved at all costs?"

"I don't know. Does it say the same with Monica?" It did. "Are there any special notations for you?"

He waited while she looked. He was not just afraid but terrified that it wouldn't have anything for her, and he would not want to contemplate living in fear for her the rest of his life. She said that it did. She looked at him, as afraid as he was.

"It says that I must be saved above all else, with the exception of my mate and children. It says that I am the one to safeguard the records." She reached for his hand. "Dylan, there's more. Are you ready for it?"

He nodded, but had wanted to shake his head. He didn't what to know what he knew, but now that he did, he also knew that it would be impossible to ever forget it. When she looked back at the computer, he held her hand.

"It says that the records are ours to keep safe at all costs. That you and I as a mated pair of panthers will live for an 'entirety,' and by doing so we'll safeguard the races against people who would harm them. We're the Keeper of the Records." She closed the computer and leaned back against him. "What does it mean to live for an entirety? Should it have been an eternity?"

He doubted it was a mistake. "Eternity means an infinite time or time without a beginning or an end. Entirety means law undivided or the sole possession. I think it means that you and I are the law governing all species."

She didn't move nor did she say anything. He waited for her to say something that would be anything he could agree with, anything other than what he'd just told her. She simply sat there for a long time and looked at the contents of the box.

"He gave us this as a prepayment to our job." He nodded. "And I wonder if we have the ability to say no. I'm thinking it's too late for that. Don't you?"

"Yes. I think the moment you and I met it was too late for that." Dylan picked up the stones and put them back in the chest, as well as the other thumb drives. "How will we know what to do about updating the information?"

"I have a feeling that it will be done for us. I have a feeling that the moment you and I have a baby...." She laughed bitterly. "Hell, probably the moment one is conceived, it will be on the records."

Dylan nodded. He watched her pull out the drive and drop it in the box with the others, and he closed it up. She put the computer on the floor and lay down. He spooned in behind her.

"I want to go home now. But I want to come back here often if you don't mind." He agreed with her. "Dylan, we'll need to figure out where to hide these things, including the jewels."

He told her he knew just the place. "You know where the place is as well. It's the only place on earth that no one but you and I, and maybe Khan, will ever know about; the wedge between the river and the stone wall."

She agreed, and they lay there together until morning. After putting the box where he'd suggested, they went home. Dylan had a feeling that things were about to get nuts. He glanced over at his wife and knew that he'd not have it any other way.

Kathi S. Barton

About the Author

Kathi Barton, author of the bestselling series Force of Nature, lives in Nashport, Ohio with her husband Paul. In addition to writing full time Kathi likes to spend time with her eight grandkids, three children and three children-in-laws. She writes to relax and have fun.

Her muse, a cross between Jimmy Stewart and Hugh Jackman brings them to life for her readers in a way that has them coming back time and again for more. Her favorite genre is paranormal romance with a great deal of spice. You can visit Kathi on line and drop her an email if you'd like. She loves hearing from her fans. aaronskiss@gmail.com.

Follow Kathi on her blog:
http://kathisbartonauthor.blogspot.com/

www.ingramcontent.com/pod-product-compliance
Lightning Source LLC
Chambersburg PA
CBHW030321180626
46810CB00003B/1185